B

Bladereaper and th
Barbarians at the
Sorcei

ɔ)

https://pjthorndyke.wordpress.com/

BAREARIANS AT THE GATES OF HOLLYWOOD:
SWORD AND SORCERY MOVIES OF THE 1980S

R **RESTRICTED** ⊛
UNDER 17 REQUIRES ACCOMPANYING
PARENT OR ADULT GUARDIAN

WARNING

This videocassette including its soundtrack is protected
by copyright.

This videocassette may be used to show the
motion picture/programme only in private homes to
which the general public is not invited and/or to
which an entrance fee is not charged.

Any unauthorised use whatsoever is prohibited.
This prohibition may be enforced by legal action.

VHS

Barbarians at the Gates of Hollywood:
Sword and Sorcery Movies of the 1980s
By P. J. Thorndyke

2020 by Copyright © P. J. Thorndyke

https://pjthorndyke.wordpress.com/

Contents

FORWARD BY THE
AUTHOR

I must have been six or seven when, while perusing the aisles of a toy store, I spotted something that set my imagination on fire. It was a box for a boardgame and its artwork depicted a muscular warrior swinging a sword in the face of a horde of goblins, his raven-black hair swinging dramatically to one side. He squatted at the foot of some steps in what looked to be an underground cavern. Two brick portals behind him hinted at a vast dungeon complex from which infinite enemies might spew forth. I was fascinated.

The game in question was *HeroQuest* made by Milton Bradley in conjunction with Games Workshop. Although I was too young to play it, or have any understanding of roleplaying boardgames, I was wholly familiar with the type of world its artwork encapsulated. I had grown up on a diet of Saturday morning cartoons like *Masters of the Universe*, *Thundercats* and *Dungeons & Dragons*. I had the He-Man toys. I pored over their box art (surprisingly grim and gloomy for a kid's toy line) and I imagined my own adventures as I hacked up patches of stinging nettles and bramble bushes behind our house with my plastic sword. I loved anything with muscle-bound warriors fighting monsters and evil magic in somber, ruined landscapes. What I saw in the *HeroQuest* box art that day both typified and distilled everything I loved about sorcery and swordplay into one image and I never forgot it.

The artwork (done by British illustrator Les Edwards) was very much of its era. Muscles were big in the 1980s. And they were big business. Bodybuilder Arnold Schwarzenegger exploded across cinema screens in movies like *The Terminator* (1984) and *Predator* (1986) while Sylvester Stallone starred in several sequels to *Rocky* (1976) as well as introducing the world to the Vietnam Vet-gone-rogue, John Rambo. The expansion of cable television ushered in a professional wrestling boom with colorful characters like Hulk Hogan and Randy Savage breaking into mainstream pop culture and becoming household names.

The fantasy genre was also affected by the image of the beefed-up macho man and similar images to the *HeroQuest* illustration could be seen in paperback spinner racks, on heavy metal album covers, comic books and movie posters. Muscles, swords, and sorcery were everywhere in the 1980s and then, as the zeitgeist evolved in the 1990s, it all vanished as if banished by a spell.

I did not know then that the raven-maned barbarian of *HeroQuest,* and everything else that resembled it, was part of a specific subgenre of literary fantasy that had a rich history going back decades, even centuries. Several elements came together in the 1980s that caused a boom in what is known as 'sword and sorcery'. In particular, the silver screen (and subsequently the video rental store) became inundated with movies that fed on a long tradition. Several big budget movies opened the floodgates for a slew of imitators, providing ample material to write a comprehensive book on.

As we shall see in the next chapter, there exists a set of definitions that sets sword and sorcery apart from other sub-genres of fantasy. This explains the absence in this book of the likes of *Excalibur* (1981) and *Ladyhawke* (1985) as well as beloved children's classics like *Willow* (1988), *Labyrinth* (1986) and *The Dark Crystal* (1982). This book instead focuses on the movies concerning individual warriors on lonely quests, the barbarian movies, the dirty, grimy, low-brow fantasy flicks aimed largely at adults who craved action, blood, nudity and a damn good time.

The purpose of the book is not to review every movie from the 1980s that has been labelled (justifiably or not) sword and sorcery. Many are either so surreal and offbeat that they defy criticism or are so downright bad that reviewing them on a basis of quality would be pointless. The charm they hold is largely borne of nostalgia and they are cherished by a select few who find in their datedness and cheap production values a certain guilty pleasure.

With perhaps the exception of *Conan the Barbarian* (1982), these movies are, at best, light entertainment and at worst, poorly-made cash-ins that wear the trappings of fantasy but in reality are little more than titillating exploitation movies only a cut above softcore porn. Most miss the point of sword and sorcery and were made without any concern for stringent genre definitions, wishing only to capitalize on current trends. They blended Star Wars style adventure with medieval romance and populated Dungeons & Dragons style settings with spaghetti western antiheroes. A better term for most of them might be 'barbarian movies' in accordance with their oiled up, shaggy-haired protagonists who, while they may claim fraternity with Conan, the resemblance is often only skin deep (if that).

The aim of this book is to comprehensively catalogue and describe all such films from a certain point in time; a specific movement of the 1980s that was so perfectly epitomized by that *HeroQuest* box art I was fascinated by all those years ago.

INTRODUCTION

"I know this: if life is illusion, then I am no less an illusion, and being thus, the illusion is real to me. I live, I burn with life, I love, I slay, and am content." - Robert E. Howard, *Queen of the Black Coast*

The term 'sword and sorcery' conjures images of a mighty barbarian warrior swinging an axe in the face of skeletal armies amidst the crumbling ruins of some lost civilization. Or an evil sorcerer intent on conquering the land through the use of his dark arts. Or perhaps a wicked cult of robed priests subjecting a naked princess to all kinds of terrors, daring a muscular hero to save her. Giant snakes, giant spiders, dragons, demons and wraiths; one might expect to see all of these depicted on a garish poster promoting a sword and sorcery movie, a genre that particularly flourished in a decade that gave us *Conan the Barbarian* (1982) and *The Beastmaster* (1982) as well as more low-budget offerings like the Roger Corman-produced Deathstalker series and the Italian-made entries like *Conquest* (1983) and the Ator saga.

But what distinguishes sword and sorcery from other sub-genres of fantasy? Why are the muscle-bound heroes and their magical quests of these films different from other fantasy films of the era like *Willow* (1988) or *Ladyhawke* (1985)? Or the likes of those titans of fantastic fiction; J.R.R. Tolkien's *The Lord of the Rings* and George R. R. Martin's *A Song of Ice and Fire*? All have swords, all have sorcery. All are set in far off imagined lands peopled with strange races, demonic beings, and brooding gods.

The Lord of the Rings has been labelled 'epic' or 'high' fantasy, and it clearly differs in content and mood to the plots of films like *Conan the Barbarian* (1982). This difference is not simply a matter of literature versus cinema with the latter being a simple tale designed to fill a couple of hours while the former is a hefty thousand-page epic telling of wars and thrones and shifting alliances. As we shall see in this chapter, the differences between these two sub-genres of fantasy lie in emphasis, motivation, and themes.

The term 'sword and sorcery' was first coined by Fritz Leiber (author of the Fafhrd and the Gray Mouser stories) in 1961 as a reply to a question posed by fellow fantasy writer Michael Moorcock (author of the successful Elric tales) as to what this genre of fiction they were writing in should be called, stating;

"I feel more certain than ever that this field should be called the sword-and-sorcery story. This accurately describes the points of culture-level and supernatural element and also immediately distinguishes it from the cloak-and-sword (historical adventure) story—and (quite incidentally) from the cloak-and-dagger (international espionage) story too!" [1]

Leiber was also playing on the term 'sword and sandal' which was used to refer to the genre of films drawing on historical, biblical, and mythological settings which was enjoying large success at that time. The phrase caught on and since then, other writers have attempted to define the term, further shaping and honing our ideas of what sword and sorcery means. Lin Carter in the forward to the anthology *Flashing Swords! #1* wrote;

"We call a story sword and sorcery when it is an action tale, derived from the traditions of the pulp magazine adventure story, set in a land, age or world of the author's invention -- a milieu in

which magic actually works and the gods are real -- a story, moreover, which pits a stalwart warrior in direct conflict with the forces of supernatural evil." [2]

Lin Carter was an influential member of SAGA (The Swordsmen and Sorcerers' Guild of America), an informal gathering of writers that also included Leiber and Moorcock as well as Poul Anderson, L. Sprague de Camp, John Jakes, Andre Norton and Jack Vance. Founded in the early sixties, this small group of storytellers promoted the genre in an era when it had largely been forgotten and are responsible for sword and sorcery being recognized as it is today.

But the sword and sorcery genre has roots that reach much farther back than Leiber's attempt to separate the action-orientated writing of he and his peers from Tolkien's saga of Middle-Earth. Indeed, it is perhaps the oldest form of story known to mankind.

The earliest literary work in the English language has been identified as *Beowulf*, a thousand-year old text written by persons unknown in England at the height of the Anglo-Saxon period. It depicts the mighty battles between its protagonist and three supernatural foes in the form of a monstrous demon called Grendel, its mere-dwelling mother and finally, a mighty dragon that terrorizes the kingdom.

The tradition of heroic storytelling goes back even further to Homer's epic *The Odyssey*, a Greek saga telling of the warrior Odysseus's ten-year return to his homeland; an adventure filled with gods, monsters, and half-mortals. The Greek myths are some of the oldest tales known to the world involving the struggle of mortals against supernatural forces with heroes such as Heracles, Perseus, Jason, and Theseus still household names more than 2,800 years on.

But even these antiquated tales of magic and sword-wielding might are surpassed in age by the *Epic of Gilgamesh*, a Mesopotamian poem preserved on a series of clay tablets that is said to be the earliest form of literary writing. In it, Gilgamesh, king of the city state of Uruk (in modern day Iraq), a being who is two parts god and one part man, embarks on a series of supernatural adventures with his companion Enkidu, a wild man created by a goddess.

Whether we refer to Odysseus and Gilgamesh of antiquity or the later struggles of Beowulf and King Arthur of the Dark Ages or the voyages of Sinbad as related in the *Arabian Nights*, we are talking about the most raw and basic ingredients of good storytelling. These tales, long before they were written down, would have been told orally, probably around a campfire that kept the shadows of darkness at bay as wide-eyed audiences listened, enraptured, as the local storyteller would relate tales of magic and heroism. To them, gods and demons existed and the gloom-haunted wilderness that surrounded their settlements presented a very real threat. Out there were monsters. Out there was *sorcery*. And the only defense these mortals had against it was their cunning, their brawn and their swords.

Such legendary epics influenced several British writers of the late 19th and early 20th centuries like William Morris who wrote *The Well at the World's End* (1896) which is seen as the first 'secondary world' novel, in that it is set in a world other than earth. Lord Dunsany's writings, considered to be the most influential early fantasy works also drew on the exotic and the magical, but, as Lin Carter stated, it was really the pulp magazines of the early 20th century that spawned the genre Leiber would later label sword and sorcery.

Cheaply made and printed on low quality 'pulpy' paper with lurid covers depicting saucy and often violent illustrations, the pulp magazines were aimed at young males who hungered for fast-paced, action-oriented tales flavored with the exotic and the fantastic. Tough-guy detective yarns were popular as were westerns and early science-fiction tales by the likes of Edgar Rice Burroughs. It was in the pages of these magazines that some of our most enduring heroes were born such as Zorro, The Shadow, Tarzan, and John Carter of Mars.

In March of 1923, an ex-journalist in Chicago by the name of J. C. Henneberger set up *Weird Tales*, a magazine devoted to the fantastic, the horrifying and the macabre. It was this magazine that showcased the work of several writers who would define the sword and sorcery genre before it even had a name. Arguably the most influential of these was Robert E. Howard whom some have named the father of sword and sorcery.

A dark and troubled Texan with a knack for energetic and gritty storytelling, Howard drew his inspiration from the earlier swashbuckling historical tales of Talbot Mundy and Howard Lamb that had graced the pages of the pulps in previous decades. His own tales of characters like Solomon Kane; the puritan adventurer of Elizabethan England, King Kull; the exiled warrior from the doomed continent of Atlantis and Bran Mak Morn; the last king of the Picts thrilled readers who yearned for more.

In 1932, Howard introduced his most famous character and one who would endure as an all-time figurehead for the genre; Conan. A mighty-thewed barbarian warrior from the savage land of Cimmeria, Conan strode across the Hyborian age, sword in hand, unperturbed by man, god or demon. Raven-haired and sullen eyed with a ferocious temper and a gloomy outlook on life, Conan is the epitome of the sword and sorcery protagonist. One of the key elements of sword and sorcery writing is perhaps best summarized in Howard's Conan tale *Beyond the Black River*;

"Barbarianism is the natural state of mankind. Civilisation is unnatural. It is a whim of circumstance. And barbarianism must ultimately triumph."

It is this segregation between barbarianism and civilization that lies at the heart of almost all sword and sorcery stories and it is a feeling that Howard was acutely aware of himself. In his writings, the evils of the world are repeatedly shown to be products of corrupt civilizations, ruled by tradition and ceremony, putrid with treachery and backstabbing. The sword and sorcery hero is one of barbaric purity, of a savage nature that hearkens back to a simpler time. He is often greeted with disdain and prejudice by the men and women of civilized lands who regard him as a brute and a savage but ultimately, it is the barbarian who emerges in the better light come the tale's end.

Howard's heroes are often men on the fringes of society, shunned by all and who in return treat society as an inconvenient hindrance. They are not out to save the world or even strive to be good men. Their existence is a constant struggle for survival in hostile environments, be they haunted jungles or crowded cities. Even if they become kings and rulers of nations (as Conan and Kull do in their later careers), their hearts yearn for something more and their minds hardly pay the people they rule a passing care.

It is these attitudes that split these characters from their counterparts in epic or high fantasy. With sword and sorcery, the struggle is usually an individual battle where the stakes are personal. In *The Lord of the Rings*, the stakes are much higher; the fate of Middle-Earth rests in the hands of Frodo and his companions. Aragorn must reclaim his birthright and save his people from the tide of darkness. Not so in sword and sorcery. There are no kingdoms to be saved in the Conan stories (or if there are, then it is for Conan's personal gain that he gets involved, not out of any sense of duty). Invariably his motivations are those of revenge, escape or simply the lust for loot.

But must a sword and sorcery protagonist be a seven-foot muscular white male with a bad temper? There are other examples. C. L. Moore, a contemporary of Robert E. Howard and a fellow *Weird Tales* contributor, wrote several Jirel of Joiry tales published in *Weird Tales* between 1934 and 1939. These presented the world with its first female sword and sorcery protagonist; a flame-haired ruler of a medieval French realm where the supernatural frequently forces itself in on her world.

Michael Moorcock's Elric of Melniboné, who made his first appearance in *Science Fantasy #47* of June 1961, has been described as something of an antithesis to Howard's giant barbarian. Born into royalty, the albino emperor Elric is a physically weak individual who must rely on special medicine to remain fighting fit.

In 1981, six short stories concerning Charles R. Saunders's Imaro character were collected and published in a paperback volume by DAW. Inhabiting the fantasy world of Nyumbani (a fictional Africa), Imaro was one of the first non-white sword and sorcery protagonists and one of the first examples of sword and sorcery by a black author.

No matter their size, sex or color, it is the unwillingness of these characters to give up and die in the face of insurmountable odds and the extraordinary situations that force them to reveal their true strengths that mark them out as heroes of the genre. They fight on because they know of no other way. To give up is to die, knowing that in all probability, the cruel and harsh world around them will barely notice their passing.

In summary, we can say that sword and sorcery differs from other sub-genres of fantasy in that it usually features an outsider character, acting out of self interest in fast-paced, episodic adventures where they must use their wits and fighting skills against evil powers in which the stakes are personal. The seminal book *Flame and Crimson: A History of Sword-and-Sorcery* by Brian Murphy acknowledges the role the pulp magazines played in the brevity of the sword and sorcery tale;

"These stories lacked the epic length of Morris' The Well at World's End or Tolkien's The Lord of the Rings. Short and episodic in nature, they matched the editorial requirements and limitations of the pulp magazine medium in which their authors worked." [3]

But, as Murphy goes on to explain, if the breezy nature of the sword and sorcery tale was a result of its pulp origins, then it quickly became a base element of the genre. Even with the advent of the mass-market paperback, sword and sorcery novels were typically short and standalone in contrast to the hefty trilogies and multi-book series of high fantasy such as David

Eddings's *The Belgariad* and Terry Brooks's *The Sword of Shannara Trilogy.*

Murphy also comments on Lou Anders and Jonathan Strahan's use of the *Iliad* and the *Odyssey* to draw a helpful comparison between high fantasy and sword and sorcery;

"High fantasy favors heroes like Hector, fighting to protect his city from outsider invaders for a larger cause; sword-and-sorcery heroes are akin to Achilles, whose preoccupation with personal wealth and feminine beauty, and the death of his friend Patrocles finally motivating him to action, are familiar to fans of the subgenre." [4]

The brevity and leanness of the sword and sorcery yarn makes it cheaper and easier to adapt to film than lengthy high fantasy tales with their large-scale battles and huge casts of characters. Perhaps in that simple economic fact we can see at least part of the reason why sword and sorcery has enjoyed a more prolific career on the big screen. But why the 1980s? As we shall see in the next chapter, the genre had been building towards a cinematic heyday for quite some time.

INFLUENCES

"I remember fans would approach me at conventions and say 'What a fabulous cover. I read the entire book awaiting to read about the scene on the cover and never found it. So I read it again thinking I missed it, but no luck.' Never judge a book by its cover." - Frank Frazetta.

Few single works of fiction have had an impact on a genre in the way that Tolkien's *The Lord of the Rings* has. Originally published as three volumes in Britain in 1954, 1955 and 1956, the books enjoyed moderate success but it was not until a decade later when U.S. publishers Ballentine released them in paperback that the world sat up and took note.

Since the demise of the pulp magazine due to paper shortages during World War Two, the fantasy and horror subject matter that had been so popular in the twenties and thirties had been driven underground. In this post-war era, science fiction emerged as the dominant form of entertainment and the names of those fantasy writers whose work had thrilled readers of *Weird Tales* and other such magazines, had been all but forgotten.

Sword and sorcery writing had continued, but in a very small way with only the occasional works of note. *The Dying Earth* (1950) by Jack Vance is one such example as is *The Sword of Rhiannon* (1953) by Leigh Brackett and L. Sprague de Camp's *The Tritonian Ring and Other Pusadian Tales* (1953). Poul Anderson, wrote two highly acclaimed novels; *The Broken Sword* in 1954 and *Three Hearts and Three Lions* in 1961 but this small and select group of authors (several of whom founded SAGA in the early sixties) was representative of the severely reduced readership of fantasy fiction at this time.

This all changed following the enormous success of *The Lord of the Rings*. Publishers suddenly realized that fantasy was a viable option and that the public was hungry for more. In 1966, U.S. publishers Lancer dusted off Howard's Conan stories (some of them having not seen print since the days of the pulp magazines) and began publishing them in paperback volumes with several stories per book. These cheap paperbacks are well known for their cover illustrations by Frank Frazetta. Brutal, brooding and violent, for many readers these paintings are the definitive depictions of Howard's barbarian hero and were one of the reasons that book sales soared.

Overseen by Lin Carter and L. Sprague de Camp, the Lancer Conan series included several pastiches by the two authors that attempted to 'complete' the saga of Conan's life which Howard had deliberately left vague. Affordable and new to many, the Lancer Conan paperbacks introduced Howard's writing to the baby boom generation who had previously been fed a diet of Cold War alien invasions and radioactive mutations. With the combined success of the *Lord of the Rings* and the Lancer Conan anthologies, fantasy was back in a big way.

The years leading up to the 1980s saw the publication of many sword and sorcery novels and stories that drew heavily on Robert E. Howard's legacy. Lin Carter's *The Wizard of Lemuria* was published in 1965 and featured the character of Thongor, a Conan-esque barbarian warrior. *Brak the Barbarian* by John

Jakes was published in 1968, shortly followed by *Kothar - Barbarian Swordsman* by Gardner F. Fox. Lin Carter was also busy at this time editing a series of anthologies for Ballentine entitled the Ballentine Adult Fantasy Series which collected out-of-print stories from the pens of William Morris, Lord Dunsany and Clark Ashton Smith among others. Karl Edward Wagner's Kane character made his first appearance in *Darkness Weaves With Many Shades* in 1970, the same year that Fritz Leiber wrote *Ill Met in Lankhmar*, the origin tale for his Fafhrd and the Gray Mouser characters whom he had first written about back in 1939. In 1973 Lin Carter edited the first issue of *Flashing Swords!*, a magazine collecting the works of the various members of SAGA and the following year marked the appearance of sword and sorcery's first black protagonist in the form of Charles R. Saunders' Imaro.

Fans of sword and sorcery fiction in the seventies had it good. As well as the ever-increasing number of paperback novels hitting the racks in newsagents and drugstores, there was another form of media to enjoy the sword-swinging, monster-slaying antics of brawny warriors.

In October of 1970, Marvel Comics published the first issue of *Conan the Barbarian*. It was a notable departure from the superhero-orientated fare of most comics of the day, but readers were clearly ready for sword and sorcery in comic book form. Written by Roy Thomas and illustrated by Barry Windsor-Smith, the comic was an instant hit. More sword and sorcery comic books followed including a more adult-orientated Conan series; *The Savage Sword of Conan* (which got around the Comics Code Authority by declaring itself a magazine, not a comic book) in 1974.

Kull – Howard's other barbarian hero – got the Marvel treatment in 1971, Lin Carter's *Thongor of Lemuria* in 1973, and *Red Sonja* was created as a female counterpart to Conan in 1977.

Hoping to steal some of Marvel's thunder, DC Comics also dipped into the genre in 1973 with *Sword of Sorcery*, a short-running series that adapted Fritz Leiber's Fafhrd and the Gray Mouser tales. More DC heroes appeared and disappeared throughout the decade such as *Dagar the Invincible*, *The Warlord*, *Stalker*, *Kong the Untamed* and *Claw the Unconquered*. Comic book and sword and sorcery fans lapped it up. As Robert E. Howard's Conan had pioneered the genre back in 1932, his most famous character had kick-started a boom in another medium over forty years later which would eventually pave the way for the genre's transition into cinema.

The deluge of fantasy fiction following the publication of the Lancer Conan paperbacks and the subsequent comic book boom inspired fans of the genre to turn to other forms of entertainment in which their own imaginations could play a part in their love for magic and monsters. In 1974 Gary Gygax and Dave Arneson released a rule system through TSR, Inc. for a role-playing game called *Dungeons & Dragons*.

In this game, the players would each take on a specific character and embark on adventures, interacting with each other and the game's inhabitants, fighting battles and collecting treasure and other artifacts. Overseeing the events is the Dungeon Master who acts as a referee and storyteller. With creatures such as elves, dragons, halflings, orcs and dwarves, Tolkien's influence is obvious but the game also drew upon the writings of many sword and sorcery writers, most notably Poul Anderson's *Three Hearts and Three Lions* in that all characters and creatures are divided into allegiances of 'law', 'chaos' and 'neutrality'. Jack Vance's *Dying Earth* was also the source of the notion that spells must be memorized and are used up once cast, requiring the wizard to re-learn them the following day. The game format was hugely successful, sweeping the U.S. like a popular cult, and inspiring a whole world of role-playing with many different variations and campaigns.

But what was the world of cinema doing during this sword and sorcery explosion? Fantasy films were nothing new, *Metropolis* (1927), *King Kong* (1933) and *The Wizard of Oz* (1939) being notable examples. But by its very definition, the fantasy genre has always been a hard one to translate to the silver screen. Whether it be mythological creatures, exotic landscapes or magical forces crackling through the air, these things all cost large amounts of money to realize on celluloid and sword and sorcery films in the decades leading up the 1980s were few and far between.

The 1950s was the era of the atom bomb and the space race; influences that swamped popular culture in the form of Martian invaders, giant radioactive bugs and flying saucers. Stop-motion effects wizard Ray Harryhausen who had cut his teeth in such sci-fi classics as *The Beast from 20,000 Fathoms* (1953), *It Came from Beneath the Sea* (1955) and *Earth vs. the Flying Saucers* (1956), had long wanted to do an Arabian Nights style adventure film and got his chance when producer and longtime collaborator Charles Schneer took an interest and promoted the idea to Columbia Pictures.

The result was *The 7th Voyage of Sinbad* (1958), a Technicolor masterpiece which featured not one of

Harryhausen's legendary stop-motion creatures but six. The huge success of the movie drew Harryhausen away from the world of science fiction and led him to be the creative force behind several other sword and sorcery adventures most famously in 1963's *Jason and the Argonauts*. Two more Sinbad features were released – *The Golden Voyage of Sinbad* (1974) and *Sinbad and the Eye of the Tiger* (1977) – with Harryhausen's effects wizardry taking its final bow in 1981's *Clash of the Titans*. But by the time Harry Hamlin's Perseus was battling Medusa and the Kraken (among others) in 1981, fantasy in cinema had really moved on. One film in particular had redefined the special effects industry and paved the way for a new breed of adventure movie for the 1980s.

Star Wars was released in 1977 to a thunderous reception. Blending the planetary romance stories of the early pulps with a brand of pseudo-Japanese chivalry and mysticism, writer and director George Lucas had created a phenomenon. *Star Wars* was an outrageously ambitious film. Its sheer scale and mind-blowing special effects combined with the age-old elements of the fairytale showed Hollywood and its audiences just what could be achieved in this modern era of filmmaking. Some have dubbed *Star Wars* 'sword and sorcery in space' and the parallels are easy to see with its exotic locations, dark lords, alien creatures, old wizards and a mystical form of sorcery known as 'the force'.

Audiences thrilled to the adventures of Luke Skywalker who, mentored by a wizened old knight of a destroyed order, sets out on an adventure to rescue a princess from the clutches of an evil lord. In the cynical post-Watergate and Vietnam era, *Star Wars* reminded people that going to the movies used to be fun. The paranoid and hysteria-mongering science fiction films of the 1950's and 1960's had died out and the trend had changed once again. The age-old adventure of mythology and magic was back on cinema screens.

THE BARBARIAN TIDE

"Crom, I have never prayed to you before. I have no tongue for it. No one, not even you, will remember if we were good men or bad. Why we fought, or why we died. All that matters is that two stood against many. That's what's important! Valor pleases you, Crom... so grant me one request. Grant me revenge! And if you do not listen, then to HELL with you!" – Conan, *Conan the Barbarian* (1982)

What the publication of *The Lord of the Rings* did for fantasy literature of the 1960s might be argued as akin to what the release of *Star Wars* did for fantasy cinema of the 1980s. While neither are solid examples of sword and sorcery, both had far reaching effects on the genre's journey from its humble beginnings in the pulps to the silver screen in the early 1980s.

In the post-*Star Wars* world of cinema, producers and studio executives were reaching out for projects that involved the fantastic, the mythic and the adventurous and, in 1981, three films were released that plumbed classical mythology and medieval romance for inspiration. While *Clash of the Titans* ushered out Ray Harryhausen's stop-motion monsters, John Boorman created what remains for many, the definitive cinematic version of the Arthurian legend in *Excalibur* and Disney's *Dragonslayer* (also set in a fantastical post-Roman Britain) brought the most realistic dragon to screens yet.

While all three films feature young men wielding swords in the face of magic and monsters, none of them really fit the definitions of sword and sorcery.

There is a fairytale element to all of them, a sense of valiant heroes doing the right thing that is at odds with the typical sword and sorcery antihero. As with Frodo Baggins, these heroes are unlikely candidates plucked from obscurity and instructed by elderly mentors to do mighty things for the good of the land. There is little of the selfish lust for gold, wine and women in Harry Hamlin's Perseus or Peter MacNicol's Galen and Nigel Terry's Arthur is prophesied to pull the sword from the stone and become king whether he wants to or not. Prophecy rarely features in sword and sorcery fiction where protagonists are the walking embodiment of free will. These films bear more similarity to high fantasy and it would fall to other films to represent that genre's wild and carefree sibling on the silver screen.

Hawk the Slayer (1980)

Director: Terry Marcel
Writer: Terry Marcel and Harry Robertson

Perhaps the first true sword and sorcery film of the decade was *Hawk the Slayer*, an early British effort from 1980. The hero Hawk (John Terry), sets out to thwart the evil Voltan (a particularly hammy Jack Palance) and his band of thugs who have kidnapped a local Abbess and are holding her to ransom. Through flashbacks, we are told that Hawk and Voltan are brothers who were once in love with the same woman. Their quarrel resulted in the young woman's death and a nasty burn which left Voltan's face permanently scarred.

As if that wasn't enough, Voltan later kills their father over the matter of their inheritance; a mystical gem known as 'the last elven mindstone'. The stone passes to Hawk who carries it in the pommel of his father's sword which imbues it with magical properties (it can fly back into its owner's hand on command).

When Hawk rescues Ranulf (Morgan Sheppard) – a refugee from Voltan's reign of terror – he learns of the abbess's plight. Guided by a blind sorceress (Patricia Quinn, best known for playing Magenta in the stage and 1975 film version of *The Rocky Horror Picture Show*) he sets about recruiting a band of mismatched heroes in true *Dungeons & Dragons* style. In addition to Ranulf and the sorceress, there is the 'giant' Gort played by *Carry On* veteran Bernard Bresslaw, Baldin the dwarf (Peter O'Farrell), and Crow the elf (Ray Charleson).

Hawk is a sword and sorcery hero of the cold-blooded type. Never showing emotion, he is more concerned with confronting Voltan than rescuing the abbess and one can't dismiss the feeling that he would gladly consign her to her fate if it meant getting even with his brother.

Hawk the Slayer is remarkably different from other entries in the genre that were to come in the following years. John Terry is no muscle-bound He-Man and he keeps his shirt (a frilly white number) on throughout. The is pre-*Conan the Barbarian* sword and sorcery and is more inspired by the tales of King Arthur than American pulp. Hawk inhabits a pseudo-medieval world where Christianity coexists with Tolkienesque creatures like elves and dwarfs which, while stalwarts of high fantasy, are usually neglected in sword and sorcery.

Set almost entirely in a damp, mossy forest with the smoke machine going full blast, this low-budget effort has become something of a cult classic partly due to its terrible special effects which involve lots of black light on ping pong balls and, in one hilarious instance, silly string.

It isn't wholly without artistic merit. Director Terry Marcel treats it as a spaghetti western, using extreme close-ups whenever Hawk faces off an opponent in a duel with an accompanying musical cue of a solitary synthesized whistle. Hawk is quite clearly the man with no name transplanted to a fantasy realm and the rapid fire of an elven longbow and staccato bursts of Ranulf's automatic crossbow are presumably an attempt to mimic the explosive shootouts of the Wild West in a world bound by medieval technology.

Akira Kurosawa's influence is evident too and not just via Sergio Leone who remade Kurosawa's *Yojimbo*

(1961) as the spaghetti western *A Fistful of Dollars* in 1964. The plot of *Hawk the Slayer* echoes *Seven Samurai* (1954) in that a village under attack by marauders employs a group of landless would-be heroes to protect them.

There is an attempt at comic relief in the tall man/short man schtick of Gort and Balin but Morecambe and Wise they are not and the humor falls a little short not to mention feeling somewhat out of place in a movie that also contains nun kidnapping, witch burning and a particularly unpleasant off-screen tongue removal. This, along with Jack Palance dispatching anybody unlucky enough to cross his path with a twist of the blade, his hideously burned face encased in a Darth Vader-esque helmet, makes *Hawk* somewhat sterner stuff than other family fantasy fare, despite being completely bloodless.

Composer Harry Robertson (who also produced and co-wrote the film with director Terry Marcel) was responsible for the music of many a Hammer horror film and for *Hawk the Slayer*, he went all out eighties synth with a disco-infused score that is at once catchy yet jarringly funky for a fantasy movie.

Despite the film's simplicity, there is a hint of a wider mythology that might have been explored. Voltan regularly pays visit to a cave to receive instruction and healing from a mysterious evil entity (the Emperor to his Darth Vader) and the closing scene sets things up for a sequel. 'Hawk the Destroyer' (as it was named by Marcel in the Fall 1980 issue of *Cinefantastique*) never came to fruition and a failed Kickstarter campaign for 'Hawk the Hunter' fizzled in 2015 meaning that Hawk and his companions are likely to remain in those damp, gloomy woods indefinitely.

The Sword and the Sorcerer (1982)

Director: Albert Pyun

Writer: Tom Karnowski, John V. Stuckmeyer (as John Stuckmeyer) & Albert Pyun

Set in the faux-medieval realm of Ehdan, a wicked usurper called Cromwell (Richard Lynch) resurrects the ancient sorcerer Xusia with the intent of overthrowing King Richard. Fearful of Xusia's powers, Cromwell does away with him once he has outlived his usefulness.

With Cromwell's forces closing in, King Richard gives his young son, Talon, his sword; a ludicrously impractical three-bladed weapon that has the added ability of shooting two of its blades as rocketing projectiles at the push of a button. When his parents are executed by Cromwell, Talon flees.

Growing up in exile to be a fearless adventurer and mercenary (played by Lee Horsley), Talon is keen for revenge. That makes two of them, for Xusia has also survived and is none too pleased with Cromwell's treachery.

A rebellion is brewing against Cromwell, led by Mikah (Simon MacCorkindale) and Alana (Kathleen Beller); the children of the late King Richard's closest advisor. When Mikah is captured by Cromwell, Alana recruits Talon to rescue him.

Talon is able to sneak into the castle via some secret passageways. He rescues Mikah using the old 'dress up as an enemy soldier' trick but is then captured himself. Cromwell has him crucified and placed at the head of a banquet during which he intends to marry Alana who he has captured.

Mikah's rebels attempt to sneak back into the castle to put a halt to Cromwell's plans but fail miserably and end up back in the dungeons. It falls to members of the king's harem (who have taken a liking to Talon) to free them and, after hilariously taking care of the jailer by pressing his face against his foot-powered grinding wheel (which he continues to operate himself), they head up to the Great Hall.

While the rebels storm the wedding feast, Talon tears himself free from his cross and unleashes hell, precipitating the final showdown with Cromwell in which the demon Xusia makes his true identity known.

The world of Ehdan with its castles, knights and feudal overlords is more reminiscent of the previous year's *Excalibur* than the ancient, pre-historic worlds of *Conan the Barbarian*. Names like 'Richard' and 'Cromwell' show that the writers plundered the history books rather than sword and sorcery literature, although the plot of an evil sorcerer brought back from the dead by a usurping tyrant and the quest of a roguish adventurer to thwart them bears some similarity to Robert E. Howard's only Conan novel *The Hour of the Dragon* (published under the title of *Conan the Conqueror* in 1950).

The movie dances between high fantasy and sword and sorcery. While Talon is undoubtedly instrumental in saving Ehdan, his main motive is revenge and, true to sword and sorcery form, wants no part in ruling the land once the final battle is over. Along with *Hawk the Slayer*, the movie can be seen as a bridge between the early fairytale-toned movies like *Excalibur* and

Dragonslayer and the post-1982 sword and sorcery movie which traded medieval romanticism for barbarian pulp.

The Sword and the Sorcerer was the debut of director Albert Pyun who would go on to make the Jean-Claude Van Damme vehicle *Cyborg* in 1989 along with many other low budget movies and direct to video fare. The makeup and effects are the movie's strongest point and, with an R certificate, Pyun was able to go all out in the horror department with gore, gooey demonic transformations and an unsettling wall of tormented faces being particular highlights.

In 2010, Pyun would direct the long-awaited sequel, *Tales of an Ancient Empire.* Lee Horsley returned but took a back seat while Kevin Sorbo (star of *Hercules: The Legendary Journeys*) played the lead, Aedan. The movie, which was promised before the credits of *The Sword and the Sorcerer,* was released directly to home video some twenty-eight years after the original. Better late than never. Or not, considering the sequel's dismal reception.

Conan the Barbarian (1982)

Director: John Milius
Wrtier: John Milius and Oliver Stone

Despite the early efforts of *Hawk the Slayer* and *The Sword and the Sorcerer*, the sword and sorcery cinematic boom would not take off until 1982 when the true hero of the genre was unleashed to cut a bloody swathe across cinema screens and spawn a slew of successors. Towering over all imitators like a bronze statue, bloody sword in hand, stands *Conan the Barbarian*, easily the best known and most popular film in the genre.

With a pre-existing fan base in the form of the readers of the Marvel comic books and the Lancer paperbacks, the idea for a Conan film had been gathering steam since producers Edward R. Pressman and Ed Summer spotted a young Austrian in a bodybuilding documentary called *Pumping Iron* (1977). Until then, Arnold Schwarzenegger's acting career had been mostly comprised of bit parts, with the exception of *Hercules in New York* (1970) in which he played the lead (albeit with his voice dubbed by another actor). His giant frame and chiseled features seemed perfect for the massive Cimmerian warrior of Robert E. Howard's tales, but it would be several years before the film would make it onto cinema screens.

The project was sold to movie mogul Dino de Laurentiis who delegated its production to his daughter Raffaella. In the interim, the script went through many changes (an early version by up and coming writer/director Oliver Stone had the story set against a post-apocalyptic backdrop peopled with mutants). Rejections and rewrites were constant and the eventual script (a collaboration between Oliver Stone and director John Milius) bore little resemblance to Howard's original tales, instead providing the character with an origin story that was lacking in Howard's yarns.

His parents killed in an attack on his village by another tribe, the young Conan is sold into slavery and then trained as a gladiator. After fighting many contests and earning a bloody name for himself, Conan is freed and sets off on his own across the Hyborian continent in search of vengeance against the evil sorcerer responsible for his parents' death.

Rescuing a chained-up thief called Subotai (Gerry Lopez), Conan and his new companion embark on a career as thieves. They attempt to steal a gem from the Tower of Serpents and meet blonde warrior woman Valeria (Sandahl Bergman), who becomes Conan's love interest. Having heard of their daring, the aging King Osric (Max von Sydow) recruits the trio to rescue his daughter who is under the sway of an evil serpent cult. Conan realizes that vengeance is within his grasp as the cult's slippery leader, Thulsa Doom (James Earl Jones, recognizable to *Star Wars* fans as the voice of Darth Vader) is the very man who killed his parents.

Despite being an original story, there are a few nods to Howard's source material; Valeria is from Howard's last Conan story, *Red Nails*, the crucifixion scene following Conan's capture by Thulsa Doom is straight out of *A Witch Shall be Born*, and the daring theft of a jewel from the Tower of Serpents bears some resemblance to *Tower of the Elephant*. Other elements were taken from the Marvel comic books rather than

Howard's writings such as the film's villain. Originally an adversary of Howard's other barbarian hero, Kull, in his story *The Cat and the Skull*, Thulsa Doom became a recurring antagonist in the Kull comics, eventually switching over to Conan's world when the Kull series folded.

Schwarzenegger played Conan with an almost childlike innocence and, with only a handful of lines in the film, the character was far removed from the quick-witted, cunning and articulate warrior of the source material. But audiences thrilled to this new hero of cinema and the film was an enormous success, not least due to Basil Poledouris's magnificent score, a brash, sweeping epic that has remained a fan favorite, often used in the promotional trailers of movies to this day.

As with the original stories, no punches were pulled by John Milius in his direction resulting in a gritty, blood-soaked film that earned an R rating upon release. Milius imbued the film with a strong Nietzschean streak; only through suffering and hard determination can Conan emerge as the *Übermensch*, a superior being that rises above the festering degeneracy of the world around him, making this a rare philosophical entry in a genre that was quickly saturated by cheap knockoffs.

The Beastmaster (1982)

Director: Don Coscarelli
Writer: Don Coscarelli and Paul Pepperman

As well as *The Sword and the Sorcerer* and *Conan the Barbarian*, a third sword and sorcery movie was released in 1982, making it a year to be remembered by fans of the genre. *The Beastmaster*, was loosely based on the 1959 science fiction novel by Andre Norton which tells the story of an ex-soldier in the future travelling to a distant planet with several genetically engineered animals with whom he can communicate telepathically.

Inspired by Harryhausen's fantasy films and the Italian 'peplum' movies such as *Hercules* (1958), Don Coscarelli (who had directed 1979's cult horror favorite *Phantasm*) chose to set the story in the distant past, a time of tribal feuds, magic and swordplay. As with Conan, the hero, Dar (Marc Singer), has his village wiped out by another tribe and sets out on a quest for vengeance.

There is the additional plot element of Dar being the lost prince of a usurped king and prophesized to slay the wicked sorcerer, Maax (Rip Torn in a prosthetic nose). Before Dar was born, Maax had a witch magically steal the baby from his mother's womb and transfer it to the birth tract of a cow. The witch led the cow out into the countryside and attempted to slaughter it but was interrupted by a wandering hunter who killed her and raised the boy as his own.

Dar grows up to have a psychic connection with animals and, after his people are slaughtered by Maax's raiders, he soon gathers some companions in the form of an eagle (providing him with a handy bird's eye view of approaching enemies), a black tiger and a pair of mischievous ferrets. With a posse guaranteed to make any audience smile, Dar sets out.

He encounters a skinny-dipping slave girl called Kiri (former Charlie's Angel and future Bond girl Tanya Roberts). After stealing her clothes and pretending to rescue her from a tiger (his animal buddies are very cooperative) he tries to persuade her to run away from her owners. She's having none of it and scampers off.

Dar continues to the city of Aruk which is dominated by a huge sacrificial pyramid. Maax has usurped Aruk's rightful ruler, King Zed (Dar's real father), and imprisoned him. Dar learns that Kiri is one of several slave girls consigned to be sacrificed. Determined to save her from this fate, Dar escapes the city and meets warrior monk Seth (John Amos) and his young charge, Tal (Joshua Milrad), the youngest son of King Zed (and therefore Dar's brother) who is in hiding from Maax.

The three of them then rescue Kiri and Dar learns that she is King Zed's niece (making her Dar's cousin which is rather unfortunate, given his feelings towards her). While Seth heads off to raise an army against Maax, Dar, Kiri and Tal infiltrate Maax's pyramid in an effort to rescue King Zed in a great *Dungeons & Dragons*-style sequence of corridors, traps and nasty green-eyed berserkers in spiky bondage gear.

Filmed for less than half the budget, *The Beastmaster* did not have the roaring success of *Conan the Barbarian*, but as with many such films from the 1980s, it has gone on to enjoy cult appeal. TV network HBO showed the film so often throughout the late '80s and early '90s that the running joke (attributed to comedian Dennis Miller) was that HBO stood for '*Hey, Beastmaster's on!*'

Coscarelli's horror leanings are evident and there are some suitably icky moments such as Dar's run-in with some vampiric bird men who envelop their victims in their leathery wings and reduce them to a pile of bones and green gloop. With a PG rating, *The Beastmaster* is a less serious and more playful successor to the brutal narcissism of Milius's Conan. Marc Singer may not have been a giant in the mold of Schwarzenegger but was much more articulate and emotive in the role of a barbarian sword swinger.

Fire and Ice (1983)

Director: Ralph Bakshi & Tom Tataranowicz
Writer: Ralph Bakshi (characters created by), Frank Frazetta (characters created by), Roy Thomas (screenplay) & Gerry Conway (screenplay)

Inspired by this first wave of sword and sorcery films, legendary animator Ralph Bakshi teamed up with illustrator Frank Frazetta to work on their own contribution to the genre.

Starting as a cel polisher at the Terrytoons animation studio, Bakshi had risen through the ranks, eventually forming his own company in 1968. His breakthrough came in 1972 with *Fritz the Cat*, (the first animation ever to receive an X certificate), based on the satirical comic strip by Robert Crumb. A string of other controversial projects followed but, in 1977, Bakshi delved into the world of fantasy with *Wizards*.

Originally titled 'War Wizards', the title was changed to avoid confusion with *Star Wars* which Twentieth Century Fox was also producing at the time (Mark Hamill took time off from playing Luke Skywalker to record a voice part). *Wizards* was an animated tale of a post-apocalyptic future where two rival wizards battle each other for control; one representing the forces of magic and the other the powers of technology.

Having no budget to animate the larger battle set pieces, Bakshi resorted to the cheaper method of tracing over footage from live action war movies such as *Alexander Nevsky* (1938), *El Cid* (1961) and *Zulu* (1964) frame by frame, creating a very realistic movement of human form. This process, called Rotoscoping, had been invented by Max Fleisher who, with his brother Dave, would later use it in their *Superman* animated shorts. Other films to use Rotoscoping include Disney's *Snow White and the Seven Dwarfs* (1937) and *Yellow Submarine* (1968).

In 1978, Bakshi followed up *Wizards* with an adaptation of Tolkien's *The Lord of the Rings*. Such a mammoth piece of work was always going to be tricky to film and the story was split into two parts. Bakshi directed the whole first part in live action and then rotoscoped the lot. The animated *Lord of the Rings* was a financially successful film, but reviews were mixed and a second part to complete the story never materialized, leaving the film in an unfortunate state of incompletion.

At this time, artist Frank Frazetta (who had famously illustrated the covers for Lancer's Conan paperbacks) was enjoying a healthy career illustrating posters for movies such as *The Gauntlet* (1977) and *Mad Max* (1979) as well as album covers for rock bands like Dust and Nazareth. Frazetta's name had become synonymous with the darkly powerful fantasy artwork that graced many book covers, magazines and album covers. A longtime admirer, Ralph Bakshi invited Frazetta to Hollywood to work on a feature-length animation that would blend Frazetta's powerful images with Bakshi's unique animation style.

The result was *Fire and Ice* (1983), an animated fantasy that follows a simple plot. The evil Queen Juliana rules the frozen fortress of Icepeak with her son, Nekron, who can control the flow of a massive glacier threatening to consume the land. Keen to secure a mate for Nekron, Queen Juliana dispatches her Neanderthal minions to abduct Princess Teegra of Firekeep.

Escaping her captors, Teegra runs into young hero, Larn, whose village has just been destroyed by Nekron's glacier. Separated from Larn by a giant octopus attack, Teegra is recaptured by Juliana's men and taken to Icepeak to be introduced to her suitor.

Teaming up with a mysterious, masked warrior called Darkwolf (a sort of cross between Batman and Conan), Larn sets off on a journey across a wild, untamed land filled with prehistoric monsters in his effort to rescue Teegra and halt Nekron and his mother's plans.

Based on ideas and characters created by Bakshi and Frazetta, the screenplay was written by Roy Thomas and Gerry Conway, both regular writers for Marvel's *Conan the Barbarian*. As with *The Lord of the Rings*, Bakshi filmed the entire thing in live action before beginning the lengthy process of rotoscoping, giving the whole film a realistic quality set against the Frazetta-inspired backdrops of ancient ruins, steaming jungles and festering swamps. Animation made it possible to show a world of epic grandeur and impressive visuals that live action films of the time simply did not have the budget for. Nevertheless, the film was not a success at the box office or with the critics who accused it of being slow and shallow. Despite the validity of these arguments, *Fire and Ice* has since become a cult classic.

Hundra (1983)

Director: Matt Cimber
Writer: John F. Goff (screenplay) (as John Goff) &
Matt Cimber (original story & screenplay)

Matt Cimber (born Matteo Ottaviano), directed
several blaxploitation movies in the seventies including
The Black 6 (1973) and *The Candy Tangerine Man* (1975).
In the early eighties, he made two adventure movies
with the athletic blonde bombshell, Laurene Landon.
One of these was the part-spaghetti western, part-
Indiana Jones cash-in, *Yellow Hair and the Fortress of Gold*
(1984). The other was a barbarian movie called *Hundra*.

While not strictly sword and sorcery (there's
precious little of the supernatural to threaten the titular
character), the film is notable for having a woman
sword-swinger in the lead, predating *Red Sonja* and
Barbarian Queen (both 1985) by a couple of years.

Laurene Landon plays Hundra, a member of a
matriarchal tribe who raise their female offspring and
give away their males. Taught to despise all men as
weak and degenerate, Hundra swears that "No man will
penetrate my body. With his sword or himself." While
out hunting, Hundra's tribe is slaughtered by men on
horseback and she is then pursued into the wilderness.

Journeying up into the mountains, Hundra makes
for the elder of her people. Despite the tribe's
contempt for men, the elder makes it clear that they will
not survive unless Hundra secures a mate and prevents
the extinction of her people.

So, however reluctantly, Hundra sets out to find a man to make her pregnant. It doesn't take long to come across the first candidate; an oafish lout who likes to play it rough. He won't do so, after beating him senseless, Hundra moves on to other prospects. She wanders into a nearby city ruled by the despotic high priest Nepakim; played by the movie's producer, Cihangir Gaffari (as John Ghaffari). Nepakim is the head of a bull cult and is abducting young women and turning them into temple harlots. Hundra doesn't think much of this and, after a thrilling rooftop chase, she falls in with her Mr. Right (literarily, by crashing through his roof).

His name is Pateray (Ramiro Olivaros) and he's a healer. Liking the look of him, Hundra demands that he mates with her. Finding this a tad forward, Pateray indicates that he likes the more refined girls the temple turns out, which is handy as a delegation of priests have turned up, ready to take Hundra in. She goes willingly and undergoes something of a makeover, hoping to impress Pateray.

The temple girls are all about pleasing the 'dominant' male. But Hundra has a few things of her own to teach them and pretty soon she is inspiring a women's lib movement. She also finally succeeds in seducing Pateray and the beastly business of conception is summarily attended to (although she doesn't seem to mind it half as much as she thought she might).

Months pass and Hundra gives birth to a daughter only for it to be snatched from her by the villainous Nepakim who hopes to blackmail Hundra into submitting to the superiority of men. You can imagine how well that goes down.

Ennio Morricone provided the score for Hundra, which is loud, operatic, and bears a striking resemblance to the score he would later compose for *Red Sonja* (1985). That is far from the only thing the two movies have in common although *Hundra* managed to be a better Red Sonja movie than *Red Sonja* ended up being. Such a favorable comparison didn't save *Hundra* from poor reviews in 1983, but its qualities have been somewhat reevaluated in recent years. It also inspired a 1988 video game developed for the Amstrad CPC, MSX and ZX Spectrum which, while providing the opportunity to leap around and hack through enemies as an 8-bit Laurene Landon, its plot bore no relation to the 1983 movie.

Golok Setan (The Devil's Sword) (1984)

Director: Ratno Timoer
Writer: Imam Tantowi

This colorful and utterly confusing entry from Indonesia stars martial artist Barry Prima who was one of the country's biggest action stars in the 1980s. He had previously starred in 1981's *Jaka Sembung (The Warrior)*, based on the comic book by Indonesian artist Djair Warni. Although that had some supernatural elements, it was ostensibly a martial arts story set in 19th century Indonesia in which its hero rebels against Dutch colonial rule.

The Devil's Sword was also based on a comic book, this time an entry in the popular 'Mandala' series by Mansyur Daman. A sword and sorcery series set in Indonesia's pre-Islamic mythological era, the wandering hero Mandala uses his martial arts to battle monsters and demons.

The movie's titular sword is forged from a meteorite by an old wizard. An object of great power, it is squirreled away in a cave and sought after by many, including the sultry Crocodile Queen (Gudi Sintara) who has a healthy sexual appetite and demands regular sacrifices. She dispatches the formidable warrior Banyujaga (Advent Bangun) to break up the wedding of a couple who have been somewhat lax with their offerings of late.

Banyujaga travels by floating rock to the wedding and unleashes hell on the assembled guests with much spurting blood and decapitated heads. The massacre is interrupted by the arrival of Mandala (Barry Prima), who fights Banyujaga, only to be thwarted by teleporting crocodile men. In the ensuing fray, Banyujaga escapes with the groom.

If this all sounds a little too bizarre, then you've got some idea of what this movie is all about. It mixes swords with sorcery, gory violence with slapstick martial arts, and throws in lasers, explosions, orgies and terrible rubber monsters for good measure. Indonesian cinema isn't known for doing things by halves.

Mandala returns to the home of his master, Abirawa, to find that Banyujaga and three other warriors have brutally tortured him. They were hoping to learn from him the location of the Devil's Sword. Brewing up a potion of mushrooms and then amputating his legs in a particularly gory scene, Mandala is able to save his master's life. Abirawa then gives Mandala a map to the mountain where the titular MacGuffin is hidden.

Mandala heads off to stop the evil foursome from getting their mitts on the Devil's Sword. On the way, he runs into Pitaloka (Enny Christina), the bride he saved earlier. She is intent on reclaiming her husband (who is currently enjoying the company of the Crocodile Queen) and joins forces with Mandala to help him find the sword.

Banyujaga and his companions arrive at the mountain before Mandala and Pitaloka do but have a falling out which results in a four-way duel. After some hacking, slashing and leaping around (and an exploding witch), only Banyujaga is left standing.

Leaving Pitaloka at the entrance to a cave, Mandala makes his way into the trap-filled lair, battling a cyclops monster on the way. He retrieves the sword but exits the mountain to find Banyujaga holding a sword to Pitaloka's throat. More chopsocky ensues (they can shoot lasers from their palms now) and Banyujaga is soundly defeated by both Mandala and Pitaloka, forcing him to teleport back to the Crocodile Queen. She is not pleased by his failure to fetch her the sword and consigns him to a fiery fate.

Mandala and Pitaloka swim their way into the Crocodile Queen's lair, aiming to slay her and rescue Pitaloka's husband. But can Mandala resist the sexual lure of the queen?

Barry Prima returned to the role of Mandala in a hard-to-find sequel made in 1987; *Mandala Dari Sungai Ular* (*Mandala from the Snake River*). There was also a 2004 TV series of the same name shown on Indonesian television.

Conan the Destroyer (1984)

Director: Richard Fleischer
Writer: Roy Thomas and Gerry Conway (story), Stanley Mann (screenplay)

With so many movies imitating *Conan the Barbarian*, it was only a matter of time before the barbarian who started it all would return for a sequel. Executive producer Dino De Laurentiis decided that the gritty and mildly philosophical adult tone of the first film would be replaced with a more kid friendly one with emphasis on action and humor that would hopefully draw in more families at the box office.

Marvel Comics writers Roy Thomas and Gerry Conway wrote the original script (titled *Conan, King of Thieves*) but were eventually replaced by Stanley Mann. Richard Fleisher was chosen to direct, mainly on the strengths of his 1958, Kirk Douglas epic *The Vikings* (which John Milius had cited as an influence on his direction of the original Conan).

Conan is joined by several new faces. Subotai, having apparently moved on to greener pastures, his chief sidekick is the thief Malak, played by Tracey Walter (who would go on to play the sidekick of Jack Nicholson's Joker in the 1989 *Batman*).

A brief attempt is made at continuity in the movie's opening scene in which Conan visits the site of Valeria's funeral pyre to pay his respects. This is interrupted by Queen Taramis of Shadizar (Sarah Douglas), who, after sending her warriors against

Conan as a test, offers him a job. He isn't interested but, after telling him that she can resurrect Valeria, he decides to hear her out.

Taramis has a niece, the petulant teenager, Jehnna (Olivia d'Abo), who is destined to restore the jeweled horn of the god Dagoth. There is a stone that can lead the way to the horn, but it can only be touched by Jehnna, meaning that the bratty princess has to come along, accompanied by her bodyguard, Bombaata (played by 7'1-foot NBA player Wilt Chamberlain).

The party pick up two more members in the form of Mako's wizard from the first movie (now given the name Akiro) and the ferocious amazon Zula (Grace Jones her first major role).

The stone is guarded by the wizard Toth-Amon in his enchanted castle (*Thoth*-Amon was a character in Robert E. Howard's Conan story *The Phoenix on the Sword* although it is unclear why his name was changed here). After sneaking into the castle, Conan is separated from his comrades and trapped in a room of mirrors where he is attacked by an ape-like monster in a red cloak (familiar to anyone who has read Howard's story *Rogues in the House* or seen the Frazetta painting it inspired).

Escaping with the jewel, the band head for the Temple of the Horn to collect the second MacGuffin but treachery is afoot. Bombaata has been instructed by Taramis to kill Conan upon retrieval of the Horn of Dagoth and carry Jehnna back to Shadizar where she is to be sacrificed upon the awakening of Dagoth. Can Conan and his companions save the princess and thwart Taramis's evil plans?

Conan the Destroyer's bloodless action and focus on goofy humor rankled with fans who enjoyed Milius's dark and brooding original. They weren't the only ones. Roy Thomas and Gerry Conway were so displeased with Stanley Mann's version of their story that they adapted their own original script (with a few name changes) into the graphic novel *Conan and the Horn of Azoth* in 1990.

Predictably, *Destroyer* did not do as well as *Barbarian*, but the film earned enough to convince De Laurentiis that there was still some money to be milked from the concept and he quickly called upon Richard Fleisher to direct a follow up as something of a Conan spin-off.

Red Sonja (1985)

Director: Richard Fleischer
Writer: Clive Exton and George MacDonald Fraser

There is often confusion surrounding the origin of the flame-haired, mail bikini-wearing character of Red Sonja, many believing her to have been created by Robert E. Howard himself. While he did create a character called Red *Sonya* of Rogatino, she was a far cry from the 'she-devil with a sword' popularized by the Marvel comics. Appearing in only one tale called *The Shadow of the Vulture* (a historical yarn set against the backdrop of the siege of Vienna), Red Sonya is a sixteenth century Eastern European whose weapon of choice is a flintlock pistol rather than a broadsword.

Roy Thomas and Barry Windsor-Smith of Marvel Comics revamped the character in 1973 (replacing the 'y' in her name with a 'j') as a female counterpart for Conan in issue #23 of *Conan the Barbarian*, placing her firmly in the Hyborian Age. Her family murdered by a band of mercenaries who then rape her, Red Sonja is visited by the goddess Scáthach who gifts her with incredible fighting skills which will vanish if she lies with a man who has not beaten her in combat. The character was popular, and she eventually got her own series in 1977.

The role of Red Sonja was originally offered to Sandahl Bergman (who played Valeria in *Conan the Barbarian*), but, keen to avoid typecasting, Bergman opted for the role of Queen Gedren, the movie's scar-faced villainess. *Hundra* star Laurene Landon was also considered but ultimately, producer De Lauentiis felt the roles were too similar and he instead plumped for twenty-one-year-old Danish model Birgitte Nielsen.

Schwarzenegger could have reprised his role as Conan, but due to problems surrounding the rights to the name, the character was changed to 'Kalidor'; Conan in all but name. That didn't stop Schwarzenegger's face featuring prominently on the poster in an effort to pull in his fans.

The movie loosely follows the comic book origins of the character, introducing Queen Gedren as the villain behind the murder of Sonja's family. This is due to Sonja spurning Gedren's sexual advances and scarring her face for good measure. Yes, Gedren is a lesbian and the presentation of her sexuality as a sign of her wickedness is a little troubling.

Years later, an order of priestesses led by Sonja's sister, Varda (who apparently left home before the massacre of her family), are attempting to banish a glowing green orb called 'the Talisman' as it has grown too powerful for them to control. Gedren and her troops arrive and steal the Talisman, sealing the priestesses in the vault which held it. Varna is able to escape (on a handy zip line) but is shot in the back by Gedren's men. She falls into the arms of Kalidor who has just arrived on the scene. Mortally wounded, she begs Kalidor to fetch her sister, Sonja, who has been training under a weapons master nearby.

Kalidor dutifully brings Sonja to her dying sister who informs her that if the Talisman is not destroyed in thirteen days, it could destroy the world. Sonja sets out to recover the Talisman, and refuses Kalidor's help. She makes for the kingdom of Hablok, which has been destroyed by the Talisman, and meets its spoiled young prince, Tarn (Ernie Reyes Jr.) and his bumbling servant Falkon (Paul L. Smith).

Queen Gedren spies Sonja's approach via a magic mirror and uses the Talisman to send a storm against her and her companions. Seeking shelter in a watery cave, they are attacked by a mechanical serpent sent by Gedren. Kalidor turns up and helps Sonja destroy the metal beast.

Before heading on to Gedren's castle, Kalidor reveals to Sonja that he is a descendant of the lords who entrusted the Talisman to the priestesses. Things get romantic and Sonja tells Kalidor about her vow at which he sensibly points out its flaw; "the only man that can have you is one who tries to kill you."

Unfortunately, De Laurentiis's securing of the rights to a cheaper property and trying to repeat the success of the Conan movies resulted in what Schwarzenegger would later call "the worst film I've ever made." *Red Sonja* bombed at the box office and has been much maligned by Conan and fantasy film fans ever since. Despite a fine score by Ennio Morricone and some fabulous production design by Danilo Donati, the movie is mired in wooden performances and the same goofy humor that plagued *Conan the Destroyer*.

Red Sonja also heralded the end of Schwarzenegger's run of barbarian movies. There was a plan for a third Conan movie to be released in 1987 called *Conan the Conqueror* but, after *Raw Deal* (1986), Schwarzenegger's contract with De Laurentiis was up and he was busy making *Predator* (1987) so the third Conan movie entered development hell where it languishes still. In 2012, Universal revived hopes by announcing Schwarzenegger's return in *The Legend of Conan*, which would be a direct sequel to the first movie, overriding the lackluster *Conan the Destroyer* but, by 2017, this project had fallen through as well.

The Barbarians (1987)

Director: Ruggero Deodato
Writer: James R. Silke (story and screenplay)

The failure of *Red Sonja* signaled something of a decline of the sword and sorcery epics that had flourished in the early part of the 1980s and *The Barbarians* was the decade's last big American entry. The remainder of the decade's output consisted largely of Roger Corman's bargain basement productions and cheapo Italian efforts, all of which are deserving of their own sections in this book.

The Cannon Group, well-known in the eighties for churning out cheap action flicks like the *Death Wish* sequels starring Charles Bronson and various Chuck Norris fare, had been bought by Israeli cousins Menahem Golan and Yoram Globus in 1979. Both shrewd businessmen, Golan and Globus became notorious for buying up bottom-of-the-barrel scripts and pre-selling distribution rights before production started, enabling them to churn out dozens of low-budget movies a year. Naturally, much of their product was b-grade schlock but the movies were cheap enough to produce that they regularly turned a profit.

Cannon's Italian production arm (Cannon Italia Srl) had already produced a couple of Hercules movies starring Schwarzenegger's old bodybuilding rival, Lou Ferrigno, and, still keen to milk the barbarian formula, Golan and Globus were looking around for new potential. The Barbarian Brothers – identical twins,

Peter and David Paul – were notorious as the 'bad boys of bodybuilding' due to their unconventional attire (denim and work boots) and playful personalities. Keen to break into the movie business, they had appeared alongside an up-and-coming Mr. T. in the Joel Schumacher film *D.C. Cab* (1983), followed by parts as lifeguards in *The Flamingo Kid* (1984). It was their appearance in the July 1986 issue of *Playgirl* dressed as barbarians, that suggested to Golan and Globus their potential as leads in a sword and sorcery flick.

A joint production between Cannon Films and Cannon Italia Srl, *The Barbarians* was helmed by Ruggero Deodato, the director behind the notorious *Cannibal Holocaust* (1980). This perhaps indicates that the movie was originally intended to be a darker, more serious piece than it ended up being. In any case, the Barbarian Brothers found the script dull and improvised a lot of scenes, playing it strictly for laughs.[5] Deodato seems to have gone with this, no doubt abandoning any hope of making a dark and adult fantasy movie with two such goofballs on board.

Peter and David play the twins, Kutchek and Gore, who have been raised in a travelling tribe of entertainers called the Ragnicks led by Queen Canary (Virginia Bryant). The evil warlord, Kadar (Richard Lynch on a villain roll after his turn in *The Sword and the Sorcerer*), attacks the troupe and begins slaughtering them. He's after a magical gem which the Ragnicks possess. The twin boys bite off a couple of Kadar's fingers and, in order to save them from Kadar's rage, Queen Canary agrees to be his willing captive. The boys are separated and sold into slavery.

Years later, Kutchek and Gore have grown into the enormous Barbarian Brothers, trained to fight to the death as gladiators. Ultimately forced to fight each other while wearing helmets that obscure their faces, the twins become aware of each other's existence when a chance blow opens Kutchek's helmet. Recognizing their respective twin, the brothers bust out of the arena and escape on some stolen horses.

Meeting up with what's left of their tribe, the twins set out with their new comrade, a thief called Ismene (Eva LaRue) who promises to help them get some weapons with which they can rescue Queen Canary. One barfight later and the trio are on their way to Kadar's palace.

Kadar is still after the magic gem, as Queen Canary was able send one of her men away with it during Kadar's raid all those years ago. It is hidden in the Forbidden Lands, guarded by a dragon. The only way to slay the dragon is with some sacred weapons from the Tomb of the Ancient King.

Such generic quest objectives are another indicator that *The Barbarians* wasn't exactly taking things seriously. Campy and daft, it wasn't the only movie of 1987 to feel like a parody of a genre that had grown a little stale (see *Deathstalker II*). While *The Barbarians* did well overseas, it failed to strike a chord with American audiences and was yet another nail in the coffin of the sword and sorcery movie.

INFLUENCE FROM
BEYOND THE STARS

*"Pathetic earthlings. Hurling your bodies out into the void,
without the slightest inkling of who or what is out here. If you had
known anything about the true nature of the universe, anything at
all, you would've hidden from it in terror."* – Emperor Ming,
Flash Gordon (1980)

It has already been noted how the release of *Star Wars*
in 1977 helped pave the way for the sword and sorcery
cinematic explosion of the 1980s, but 'sword and
planet' (and to a lesser extent, planetary romance) has
been a kindred genre to sword and sorcery since the
earliest days of the pulps. One of the greatest writers of
pulp fiction is undoubtedly Edgar Rice Burroughs. His
character, Tarzan, is one of the great heroes of pop
culture but it is one of his less famous creations that has
influenced both science fiction and sword and sorcery
writers for decades.

Inspired by Edwin Lester Arnold's 1905 novel,
Lieut. Gullivar Jones: His Vacation, Burroughs wrote his
own tale of a military earthman who journeys to Mars
and falls in love with a princess. John Carter of Mars
first appeared in the serialized novel *Under the Moons of
Mars* (later published as *A Princess of Mars*), in *All-Story*
Magazine in 1912. A civil war veteran who is bodily
transported to the red planet by some mystical power,
John Carter finds himself in a world that is at once
high-tech and yet brutally savage, a landscape of
crumbling civilizations and harsh, exotic terrain. The

combination of swashbuckling swordplay with high-tech innovations like radium pistols and flying machines lies at the heart of sword and planet, a fusion of science fiction and medieval-style derring-do.

Sword and planet grew in popularity as the pulp era progressed with many imitating Burroughs' style and ideas such as Otis Adelbert Kline who wrote *The Swordsman of Mars* in 1933. Kline also allegedly completed Robert E. Howard's own sword and planet adventure, A*lmuric*, which was posthumously serialized in Weird Tales in 1939.

In 1934, King Features Syndicate asked young cartoonist Alex Raymond to come up with a Sunday newspaper strip that could rival the success of *Buck Rogers*, a strip in the National Newspaper Syndicate of America. The result was *Flash Gordon*, an enormously popular series that told of an athletic young polo player who is kidnapped along with love interest, Dale Arden, by an eccentric professor called Dr. Hans Zarkoff. Blasting off into space aboard Zarkoff's home-made rocket ship, the trio crash land on the planet Mongo ruled by the evil Emperor Ming. The series spawned three movie serials, two radio serials, a live action TV series, a Saturday morning cartoon and numerous comic books and novels.

While both sword and planet and planetary romance share a common origin in Burroughs, marked differences emerged as the two subgenres evolved. Sword and planet tales of men from earth winding up on other worlds, or even future versions of Earth, such as Leigh Brackett's *The Sword of Rhiannon*, Andre Norton's *Witch World* and John Norman's *Gor* series were never as heavy on the science as other subgenres of science fiction. As with *Star Wars*, which they would later influence, adventure and action take precedence over the laws of physics with the exotic planets simply a backdrop for a story that might just as easily take place in the Wild West or the ancient world.

Planetary romance tales, while undoubtedly overlapping somewhat with sword and planet, are generally more self-contained stories concerning the fate of the planets themselves and featuring no time travelling protagonists. The large cast of characters and intricate political powerplays of Frank Herbert's *Dune* or Anne McCaffrey's *Dragonriders of Pern* series make them more akin to high fantasy while the breezy, intimate adventures of the lone protagonist of the sword and planet genre make it a kindred spirit to sword and sorcery.

Flash Gordon (1980)

Director: Mike Hodges
Writer: Lorenzo Semple Jr.

Dino De Laurentiis had held the rights to Flash Gordon for many years, hoping that Federico Fellini would be eventually convinced to direct it. George Lucas had tried to buy the rights from him but Dino wasn't selling and Lucas went off to do his own interplanetary adventure that stylistically borrowed from Alex Raymond's strip and in particular the movie serials starring Buster Crabbe[6].

The project eventually went into production with a script written by Lorenzo Semple Jr. who had been behind the campy 1966 *Batman* live action TV series and had also penned the 1976 *King Kong* remake for De Laurentiis.

Flash Gordon has become a camp classic, loved for its ropey special effects, inherent silliness and over-the-top garishness. Directed by Mike Hodges (who had helmed the classic British crime caper *Get Carter* in 1971), the parts of Flash and Dale Arden were filled by newcomers in the shape of former U.S. Marine and Playgirl centerfold model Sam J. Jones and Melody Anderson. The rest of the cast boasted an impressive gallery of well-known thespians including Max von Sydow as Emperor Ming and Topol as Dr. Zarkov.

Ming, the bored ruler of the planet Mongo, amuses himself by slowly destroying planet Earth by successive waves of natural disasters. Flash, now updated from a polo player to a quarterback who wears his own nickname on his t-shirt, clambers abord a small plane with travel agent Dale Arden. The plane is struck by a meteorite and crash lands in the grounds of Dr. Hans Zarkov's laboratory.

Zarkov believes that the natural disasters are the result of extraterrestrial forces and has secretly constructed a rocket ship. Luring Flash and Dale onboard, Zarkov launches the rocket which then crashes on the planet Mongo.

Captured by the forces of Emperor Ming, Flash, Dale and Zarkov are taken to Ming's castle where Dale is added to the royal harem, Zarkov is scheduled to be reprogrammed and Flash is sentenced to death. Ming's daughter, Princess Aura (Ornella Muti), has taken a liking to Flash and helps him escape. They flee to Aura's lover, Prince Barin (James Bond-to-be Timothy Dalton), who is Mongo's true heir.

Captured by the Hawkmen who are led by Prince Vultan (Brian Blessed), Flash and Barin are taken to Sky City where they are forced to fight each other. Flash refuses to kill Barin and the tournament is interrupted the arrival of Ming who, impressed by Flash, offers him a job as overlord of Earth. Flash isn't interested and instigates a rebellion against the tyrant.

As he would do with *Red Sonja* five years later, production designer Danilo Donati pulled off a stunning job. Mongo is a world of vivid colors and garish designs perfectly complementing its 1930's newspaper strip origins. The soundtrack was provided by Queen (one of the first times a rock band scored a big budget movie), their title song 'Flash' becoming indelibly synonymous with the movie.

Unfortunately, the film was not a commercial success in the U.S., although it fared significantly better with British audiences who recognized its many stars (and perhaps enjoy high camp more than Americans). Another, more ironic possibility for its failure, may have been the success of *Star Wars* and its hugely popular sequels, the first of which – *The Empire Strikes Back* – was released six months previously. *Star Wars* had shown that the sword and planet genre that had been out of fashion for a couple of decades could be done and done well in the modern era of filmmaking, making this campy take on one of its greatest characters somewhat redundant.

Prisoners of the Lost Universe (1983)

Director: Terry Marcel
Writer: Terry Marcel and Harry Robertson

Fans of *Hawk the Slayer* (1980) should probably check out Terry Marcel's science fiction follow up, *Prisoners of the Lost Universe* for which he reunited with fellow writer Harry Robertson. Once again, Robertson composed the score, a far more traditional swashbuckling piece than his previous synthesized disco effort.

Opening in present day Los Angeles, TV presenter Carrie (Kay Lenz), is on her way to visit the eccentric scientist, Dr. Hartmann (Kenneth Hendel), who has developed a matter transmitter. On the way, an earth tremor nearly causes a collision between Carrie and an electrician named Dan (Richard Hatch from the original *Battlestar Galactica* series). Dan's truck is run off the road and they argue about whose fault it was. Dan is also a champion kendo fighter (which will surely come in handy later) and he is most displeased that his bamboo sword has been broken. Carrie doesn't have time for this and she speeds off to her appointment, leaving Dan stranded by the roadside.

While demonstrating his machine for Carrie, Dr. Hartmann opens up a portal to another dimension but another of those pesky earth tremors sends him tumbling through it. Dan the irate electrician arrives at the house looking for car assistance. Instead he finds Carrie all alone and he doesn't believe her story of the vanishing scientist one bit. But he's about to, as another tremor sends both him and Carrie through the portal.

Finding themselves in a primitive world peopled by strange mutants, the squabbling pair are forced to team up as they are pursued by humanoids with glowing red eyes. Helped out by a friendly caveman, Dan and Carrie free the mutants' captive; a green-skinned man called simply, 'the greenman' (Ray Charleson who played the elf in *Hawk the Slayer*.

Desperate to get back to their own world, Dan and Carrie set out in search of Dr. Hartmann. Carrie is captured by local warlord Kleel (John Saxon) whose position of authority is presumably due to his possession of an 18th century flintlock pistol with which he shoots Dan and leaves him for dead.

Apparently only grazed, Dan meets scampering rogue Malachi played by Peter O'Farrell (another *Hawk* alumnus playing pretty much the same character here) who takes him to a cave tavern to purchase some horses. Dan spots the greenman being plied with drink and tries to enlist his help. Following the obligatory bar fight, they flee on horseback.

Pursued by the bar's angry patrons, Dan, Malachi and the greenman are captured and Dan is made to fight a gold-skinned giant. He wins (by kicking him in the nuts, which make a loud metallic 'clang') and the gang are forced to fight their way to freedom. Now armed with a sword, Dan intends to put his kendo skills into practice and rescue Carrie.

Meanwhile, Carrie has been brought to Kleel the Warlord's fortress where she finds that Dr. Hartmann is in Kleel's employ, making weapons for him. Time being different in this parallel universe, the doc has been here for over a year and has happily been supplying the bad guys with explosives which makes Dan's rescue attempt somewhat tricky.

About the same level of quality as *Hawk the Slayer*, *Prisoners* hasn't become a cult classic to the same extent. Not exactly shot as a comedy, the tone of the movie is often confused by the cartoonish sound effects that regularly punctuate the proceedings. As in *Hawk the Slayer*, Terry Marcel didn't go in for a muscular barbarian protagonist. Dan is thoroughly average-looking as far as sword-swinging heroes go. He's also probably the only sword and sorcery hero who wears a plaid shirt throughout.

Il Mondo di Yor (Yor, the Hunter from the Future) (1983)

Director: Antonio Margheriti (as Anthony M. Dawson)

Writer: Juan Zanotto and Ray Collins (graphic novel "*Henga, el cazador*"), Robert D. Bailey and Antonio Margheriti (as Anthony M. Dawson) (screenplay)

Argentine comic book character, 'Yor the Hunter', created by Eugenio Juan Zappietro and Juan Zanotto, first appeared in the weekly comic anthology magazine *Skorpio* in 1974. Directed by the Italian low budget movie maestro, Antonio Margheriti, *Yor, the Hunter from the Future* was originally planned to be a four-part TV miniseries broadcast on RAI Radiotelevisione Italiana. The movie ended up being released theatrically and was trimmed down from its Italian cut by nine minutes for American audiences when it was picked up and distributed by Columbia Pictures.

Reb Brown (who was Captain America in a couple of TV movies made in 1979) stars as Yor, a haystack-bewigged prehistoric hunter who wanders a desert landscape peopled by cavemen and dinosaurs. Rescuing cave girl Kala (*Moonraker* Bond girl and titular star of *The Story of O*, Corinne Cléry) and her elderly companion, Pag (Luciano Pigozzi) from a dinosaur attack, Yor is befriended by their tribe. They note that Yor wears a strange metal medallion around his neck, the twin of which, an elder notes, is worn by 'the daughter of the gods' who is worshipped as a queen on the other side of the mountains.

During a celebratory feast, the village is attacked by a more primitive, blue-faced tribe. Yor and Pag escape and track the enemy to their lair where Yor rescues Kara by killing a giant bat and constructing a hang glider from its corpse. Agreeing to help Yor learn the secret of his origins, Kara and Pag accompany him on a quest across the mountains.

The 'daughter of the gods' is located and her name is Roa (Ayshe Gul in her only screen role). It's not just the medallion that she and Yor have in common. Both are unusually blonde and Yor surmises that they are of the same lost race. Roa is queen of the sand people, although the position seems to be purely ceremonial as she is little more than their prisoner. Yor slaughters everybody and he and Roa escape.

Roa doesn't make it very far, slain in another caveman attack. As she dies in Yor's arms, she reveals to him that memories have returned to her of an island which is the home of their people.

Contact with a friendly tribe (after another dinosaur fight) is abruptly spoilt by attack by invisible spaceships that blast everything to pieces with lasers. This sudden appearance of advanced technology (along with the movie's title) may give you a clue as to what the big 'twist' turns out to be.

Yor and his companions depart in a boat and are shipwrecked on a strange island ruled by a futuristic society. It is at this point that the movie enters *Star Wars* territory complete with a dark lord and his army of black clad androids in samurai-inspired helmets. Yor learns that a cataclysmic nuclear fallout reduced the planet to its primitive state *Planet of the Apes* style.

Yor, the Hunter from the Future did surprisingly well given its bargain-basement production values, grossing more than two-million dollars in the states, causing Antonio Margheriti to refer to it as "one of the most successful pictures of my life"[7]. Critics panned it for being cheap, tacky and cheesy, all of which is true, and the movie is hardly helped by the snappy disco theme song with the repetitive chorus; *"Yor's world, he's the man!"* which was nominated for a Golden Raspberry Award for Worst Original Song in 1983.

Highlander (1986)

Director: Russel Mulcahy

Writer: Gregory Widen (story & screenplay), Peter Bellwood and Larry Ferguson (screenplay)

Inspired by Ridley Scott's *The Dualists* (1977) as well as a summer vacation in Scotland, film student Gregory Widen wrote the original script for *Highlander* as a class assignment at UCLA which he then sold for $200,000. Thorn EMI approached Australian music video director Russell Mulcahy with the project, then called 'The Dark Knight'. After seeing a picture of Christopher Lambert in *Greystoke: The Legend of Tarzan, Lord of the Apes* (1984) in a magazine, Mulcahy knew he had found his immortal Scotsman.[8]

Highlander tells the tale of the Immortal, Connor MacLeod (Lambert), who is an antiques dealer in present day New York. Followed into a dimly lit garage by a man in a trench coat, the two fight and Connor beheads him with a samurai sword. He is arrested but later released.

Brenda Wyatt (Roxanne Hart) is a forensic scientist and expert in metallurgy working with the police. Extracting fragments of Connor's sword embedded in a concrete pillar in the garage, she deduces that they came from a 7th century Japanese sword but made with medieval technology. By investigating Connor, she finds that he has been alive for centuries, occasionally faking his own death and assuming the identities of children who had died at birth.

Through a series of flashbacks, we learn Connor's tragic tale. Originally a Scottish warrior from the 16th century, he survives a mortal blow from an enemy clan leader known as 'The Kurgan' (Clancy Brown). Convinced his miraculous recovery is the work of the devil, Connor's clan exile him, and he eventually settles down as a blacksmith with his wife Heather (Beatie Edney).

Visited by the strange and colorful wanderer, Ramirez (Sean Connery), Connor learns the truth; he and Ramirez are Immortals who can only be killed by decapitation. Eventually, all the Immortals will take part in a tournament called 'The Gathering' in which there will be only one survivor (hence the movie's tagline 'There can be only one'). The survivor will be granted 'The Prize' which is unlimited knowledge of the universe.

Ramirez trains Connor in sword fighting but is slain by the Kurgan who is also an Immortal. Determined to win the Prize, the Kurgan tracks Connor in the present day and kidnaps Brenda (who has become Connor's lover) in an effort to draw him out and slay him.

After their acclaimed work on *Flash Gordon* (1980), Queen were contacted to provide a song for *Highlander*. They loved the provided 20-minute reel so much that they turned in three tracks; "A Kind of Magic", "Princes of the Universe" and "Who Wants to Live Forever", the last of which featured an orchestra conducted by Michael Kamen who also scored the movie (8).

Highlander was not a box office success and was poorly received by critics. However, like *Flash Gordon*, it performed better in Europe where it had a 116-minute running time as opposed to the U.S. version which had been cut by roughly eight minutes. It did far better on home video and became a cult classic, launching a long-running franchise including four filmed sequels, three TV series, an anime movie and a slew of novels and comic books.

Masters of the Universe (1987)

Director: Gary Goddard
Writer: David Odell

1987 saw the notorious Cannon Films attempt to bring audiences 'The *Star Wars* of the 80s' with *Masters of the Universe*, the highly anticipated motion picture of the phenomenally successful Mattel toy line and accompanying Filmation cartoon.

For over half a decade, children across the world had been wrapped up in the adventures of the mighty-muscled He-Man and his fellow denizens of the planet Eternia, a post-apocalyptic world where swords meet laser gun technology, as they try to prevent the evil Skeletor from gaining control of Castle Grayskull, the key to ruling the universe. It was one of the first instances of a cartoon based on a toy line rather than the other way around and sales of Mattel's ever inventive action figure line dominated the competition in the toy industry. It was sword and sorcery against a science fiction backdrop for its youngest audience yet, a sort of a cross between *Conan* and *Star Wars*.

An urban legend has persisted for many years that Mattel had originally intended to produce a series of action figures based on *Conan the Barbarian* (1982), but upon seeing a rough cut of the movie with its gore and sex, decided that perhaps a toy line wasn't such a great idea after all. Not wanting the designs and prototypes to go to waste, the line was hastily modified into He-Man and the Masters of the Universe. This rumor has since been put to bed. Conan and the Frazetta paintings were clearly an influence on the design of He-Man and Mattel *did* negotiate a licensing agreement to make toys based on *Conan the Barbarian*. However, it was made clear when Mattel was sued for copyright infringement (a case Mattel won), that He-Man had been in existence as a separate planned toy line before such negotiations took place.[9]

The action figures were originally packaged with mini-comics that developed the backstory for He-Man and his associates. A wandering barbarian from a jungle tribe, He-Man battles Skeletor for two halves of the magical Power Sword which can unlock the secrets of the universe. This is markedly different from his origin in the Filmation cartoon (ostensibly devised as a marketing tool for the toys) in which He-Man is the superhuman alter ego of the mild Prince Adam of Eternia. Here, the Power Sword is given to Adam by the Sorceress of Grayskull, and is the means by which Adam transforms into He-Man.

Edward R. Pressman (who was a producer on both Conan movies) saw the potential in a *Masters of the Universe* movie and orchestrated a deal between Mattel and Cannon Films in which both parties would finance 50% of the picture each. Cannon was in financial trouble and Golan and Globus were pursuing a risky strategy to save it by buying up well-known intellectual properties that were currently out of favor (like Superman and Spider-man), and banking heavily on their ability to turn them into successful feature films.

Muppet Show writer David Odell (who also wrote 1982's *The Dark Crystal* and 1984's *Supergirl*) penned the script and Gary Goddard (who had designed the Universal Studios attraction *The Adventures of Conan: A*

Sword and Sorcery Spectacular) was called in to direct. Swedish martial artist and *Rocky IV* villain, Dolph Lundgren starred as He-Man and Frank Langella as Skeletor.

Using a stolen cosmic key, Skeletor captures Castle Grayskull and its sorceress. The key is the work of the dwarfish locksmith and inventor, Gwildor (Barry Barty) who, luckily, possesses a prototype. He-Man and his brave resistance fighters, sneak into Castle Grayskull and attempt to rescue the Sorceress but are forced to flee through a portal using Gwildor's prototype.

They find themselves on Earth in the 20th century but, having lost the cosmic key, begin a desperate search. The key has fallen into the hands of two local teenagers; Julie (Courtney Cox) and her boyfriend Kevin (Robert Duncan McNeill, who played Tom Paris in *Star Trek: Voyager*). Accidentally sending out a signal from the cosmic key, Julie and Kevin unwittingly alert Skeletor to the key's location.

Skeletor sends his minions, including an army of Darth Vader look-alike androids (created so Dolph Lundgren would have some enemies to hack through as Mattel demanded that He-Man refrain from actually killing anybody), to Earth to retrieve the key. He-Man is captured and brought back to Eternia in chains to witness Skeletor's transformation into the Master of the Universe.

The movie skewed closer to the original mini-comics rather than the cartoon, as there is no mention of Prince Adam or the royal family of Eternia and Dolph Lundgren plays He-Man throughout. However, fans were disappointed to find their favorite characters redesigned beyond recognition or absent entirely in a movie that spent more time on Earth than Eternia.

Masters of the Universe bombed upon release, largely due to Cannon running out of money to promote it or even complete it properly. Another contributor to its failure was that interest in He-Man and his companions had waned by 1987. Unbeknownst to the filmmakers, the toy line was on its last legs with Mattel reporting heavy losses. The movie came too late and, coupled with Cannon's other great flop of 1987 (*Superman IV: The Quest for Peace*), the company was in trouble.

Plans for a sequel to *Masters of the Universe* as well as a Spider-man movie fizzled as Cannon were unable to keep their licensing deals with Mattel and Marvel. Existing sets and ideas from both projects were hastily reshuffled into the Albert Pyun-directed film *Cyborg* (1989) starring Jean-Claude Van Damme.

Gor (1987)

Director: Fritz Kiersch
Writer: Rick Marx & Harry Alan Towers (as Peter Welbeck) (screenplay)

With Cannon now in serious financial trouble, Golan and Globus continued to plough ahead, refusing to slow down and lick their wounds. As well as Superman and Masters of the Universe, they also took a less-risky chance on adapting the first book in the fairly unknown although highly controversial Gor series.

Written by philosophy professor John Frederick Lange Jr. under the pseudonym 'John Norman', The Gor saga tells of the distant planet of Gor, a world where technology is regulated by the insectoid Priest-Kings who keep the human population in a state of primitive barbarity. Using Edgar Rice Burroughs as a springboard, the early books (begun in 1966) concern the adventures of Earthman Tarl Cabot, a history professor who is mysteriously transported to Gor. Here he discovers a world of rigid caste-systems where women are slaves to men and Social Darwinism reigns supreme.

The books have become notorious for their running theme that, not only are women chained and branded as the property of men, it is an arrangement most of them see as the rightful and natural way of things. Protagonist Tarl Cabot also embraces this philosophy, stating in *Beasts of Gor* that "Every organism has its place in nature. That of woman is at the foot of man." There *are* free women on Gor, but these are usually mothers and sisters who remain chaste and sexually repressed. If such a woman shows a smidgen of sexual desire for a man, it is taken as a sign of her desire to submit to him and she is summarily striped of her freedom and made a slave.

Despite drawing widespread condemnation, the books currently number thirty-five volumes and have retained a loyal, but relatively underground following. They have also inspired a subculture in which some fans (both male and female) identify as 'Goreans' and adopt a 'Gorean lifestyle', practicing female slavery in their everyday lives.[10]

Cannon's 1987 film titled simply *Gor*, was produced by Harry Alan Towers. Towers had just produced a sword and sandal flick called *Warrior Queen* (1987), which borrowed heavily from the Roger Corman-produced *Barbarian Queen* (1985), right down to its Boris Vallejo illustrated poster. He had also written the script for Cannon's *Lightning, The White Stallion* (1986) which was enough to convince Golan and Globus to pair him with their man in South Africa, Avi Lerner.[11]

Avi Lerner had been in South Africa for a few years and had produced several movies and owned a chain of movie theatres. Cannon had recently set up shop in Johannesburg, purchasing Lerner's theatre chain and making him vice president of Cannon International. Not only did South Africa offer stunning landscapes uninterrupted by powerlines and other traces of modernity (making it perfect for historical backdrops, or in *Gor*'s case, alien planets), but, most importantly for companies on the lower end of the scale, it was *cheap*.

But working in apartheid South Africa was not something movie studios were keen to advertise, as there was strong condemnation of any perceived financial support of its regime. The Motion Picture Association of America supported a cultural boycott and Cannon's San Vincente Boulevard offices were picketed by American and South African protest groups.[12] But the country offered prospects too attractive for the likes of Cannon to pass up. Feeling the squeeze of international trade sanctions, the South African government was keen to attract foreign movie producers and introduced tax concessions on the export of films making it something of a tax haven.[13]

Avi Lerner had already put South Africa's stunning scenery to use in a sequel to Cannon's *King Solomon's Mines* (1985) and made it double as a Caribbean island in *American Ninja 2: The Confrontation* (1987). The same trick would be pulled off in partnership with Harry Alan Towers in adapting a couple of Rupert Gilchrist's *Dragonard* novels, as well as making it stand in for the arid planet of Gor.

The plot of *Gor* bears little resemblance to *Tarnsman of Gor* (the first book in the series) other than its very basic premise. Tarl Cabot (played here by Italian actor Urbano Barbarini) is a hapless professor who gets dumped by his girlfriend for a young Arnold Vosloo in killer shades and a jeep. While driving through a thunderstorm to the tune of *Ruby Dawn* (the song from the end credits of *The Barbarians* which Cannon conveniently already had the rights to), he crashes into a tree and wakes up on the planet of Gor.

He witnesses a raid on a village by the ruthless tyrant Sarm (a half-naked Oliver Reed in a career slump that saw him sign on for six movies with Harry Alan

Towers). Sarm steals the village's Home Stone and captures its chief, Marlenus (Larry Taylor). Tarl, klutz that he is, accidentally kills Sarm's son and is welcomed as a hero by the fleeing villagers. Sarm is less than pleased, ordering a hundred men, women and children to be tortured until Tarl's capture.

Despite quickly realizing that Tarl is a bumbling ass, the villagers are convinced he is some sort of savior due to a mystical ring he wears. Thus begins a Rocky-style montage in which Tarl is trained in the use of the native weapons. Judging him ready, the village elder and two warriors – Talena, daughter of the captured chieftain (Rebecca Ferratti) and Torm (Rufus Swart) – accompany Tarl on a journey across the desert to the Mountains of Sardar where they intend to reclaim the Home Stone and rescue Marlenus.

Jack Palance provides occasional snippets of voice over throughout the movie and appears in the final scenes as Xenos; a priest come to guard the recovered Home Stone. Just before the credits roll, he discloses to the audience his plan to rule Gor as well as his fears of being thwarted by Tarl Cabot of Earth.

Directed by Fritz Kiersch (whose most famous movie is 1984's *Children of the Corn*), the film does make an attempt to throw in a few character names from Norman's novel, even if the characters in the film bear no resemblance to their literary counterparts and the heroic character of Tarl Cabot is reinvented as a hopeless loser who spends most of the film tripping over his own feet.

There are no insectoid aliens or flying 'tarns'; apparently victims of the movie's meagre budget which also did for Gor's sprawling cities, here rendered as generic dusty desert towns. Gor's caste system of masters and slaves (a defining aspect of the novels) is also done away with aside from the fact that Sarm takes people as slaves (as evil warlords generally do). Tarl in fact leads a rebellion against the evils of slavery which is as about as far from the books as you can get but perhaps most distressing of all to fans of John Norman's work was the film's PG rating, ensuring that the world of Gor with its BDSM undertones and violent bloodletting was significantly toned down.

Outlaw of Gor (1989)

Director: John 'Bud' Cardos
Writer: Harry Alan Towers (as Peter Welbeck) & Rick Marx (screenplay)

Rather surprisingly, Jack Palance made good on his promise of a sequel as one did indeed follow, this time produced by Breton Film Productions (which producer Harry Alan Towers set up to produce his South African productions with Avi Lerner). Cannon presented the final product, having pulled out of South Africa in 1989 due to threats of a boycott from film industry and political groups opposed to apartheid.[14]

Director Fritz Kiersch was replaced by John 'Bud' Cardos, who is something of a jack-of-all-trades in Hollywood, having been a stuntman, actor and director as well as an uncredited 'bird wrangler' on Hitchcock's *Psycho* (1960) and *The Birds* (1963).

Tarl Cabot, after returning to Earth at the end of the previous movie, is bored stiff and reduced to hanging out at a hotel bar while his odious friend, Watney (Russel Savadier), tries unsuccessfully to pick up girls. We are given a glimpse into Tarl's gloomy reverie via a montage of scenes from the previous movie that serves as a recap. While driving Watney to another bar, Tarl's ring starts to glow and, once again, he is whisked off to Gor for another adventure, this time with an annoying sidekick.

After fending off an attack by some desert warriors, Tarl and Watney make their way to the city of

Koroba where Tarl is welcomed back with open arms by Marlenus (Larry Taylor again) and his people. One person who is less than pleased by Tarl's return is Lara, Marlenus's wife (Donna Denton). Make that two people, as Lara is in cahoots with the high priest, Xenos (Jack Palance) who wants to rule Koroba himself.

Rebecca Ferratti is back as Marlenus's daughter, Talena, and she's not too happy with her new stepmom. And with good reason, for during Tarl's homecoming festivities, Lara poisons and stabs Marlenus. Tarl, upon discovering the king's corpse, is framed for his murder. Watney is no help as he provides Lara with a false alibi, having been promised by her that he can co-rule as her lover. Some friend. Talena doesn't believe a word of it and is thrown in prison while Tarl and Hup the dwarf (a companion from the first movie) escape the castle.

Tarl and Hup make their way to a nearby town and cause a ruckus in the slave market, riding off with a piece of the merchandise. Keen to please her new 'master', the slave girl offers herself on a plate to Tarl who politely declines as he is in love with Talena.

Seized in their sleep by a bounty hunter, the trio are marched back to Koroba. Tarl is brought before Lara who, much to Xenos's dismay, does not execute him on the spot. Lara wants Tarl to confess to the murder of Marlenus but no amount of whipping will make him do so. In frustration, she orders him to die in the arena with Talena chained to a pillar, watching on.

Cannon was heavily in debt by this point and, with their big franchise movies falling flat at the box office coupled with an investigation by the U.S. Securities and Exchange Commission into their financial reports, the company was on the rocks. Italian financier, Giancarlo

Parretti, swooped in and bought the company from Golan and Globus (along with the French studio Pathé), and renamed it Pathé Communications.

Not seeing eye to eye with their new owner or his own cousin, Golan left the company and formed 21st Century Film Corporation while Globus remained with Pathé and continued to produce films under the Cannon logo. The two cousins would not speak to each other again for several years.

This split resulted in one of the most bizarre bouts of studio rivalry in Hollywood history. Keen to capitalize on the 'Lambada' dance craze begun by Kaoma's 1989 hit single, Golan and Globus had planned a Lambada movie together. Now, both parties raced to be the first to get the movie made resulting in two competing projects; Globus's *Lambada* and Golan's *The Forbidden Dance*. Both were released on March 16th, 1990 with limousines from both groups arriving at the same theatre while the movies split box office profits between them.[15]

ROGER CORMAN TAKES A STAB

"I steal and kill to stay alive. Not for the luxury of Glory."
– Deathstalker, *Deathstalker* (1983)

In the world of low budget filmmaking, one name stands taller even than Golan, Globus and Cannon Films; Roger Corman. Often following trends but sometimes setting them (as with *The Wild Angels* in 1966 which preceded *Easy Rider* by three years), Corman is famous for producing movie after movie with as little expense as possible. He also has a reputation for shooting movies at an extraordinarily fast pace, in some cases completing them in a matter of days and often using the same sets and camera equipment to shoot two movies for the price of one. Having directed over fifty movies and produced a staggering five-hundred and fifty, Roger Corman's name is a byword for productivity in the business, if not for quality. He has been dubbed by many as 'King of the b-movies', although this is somewhat inaccurate as the era of the b-movie died out at the end of the 50's despite the term remaining synonymous with low budget, low quality cinema to this day.

Born in 1926, Detroit, Michigan, Corman rose to prominence in the era of the drive-in movie theatre, when America's fears of the bomb, communism and teenage delinquency were played out on the big screen. His first produced feature was *Monster from the Ocean Floor* (1954), the first of many science fiction monster movies he would direct throughout the fifties along with forays into other genres including westerns, gangster flicks, and teenage rock 'n' roll movies.

During the sixties he became famous for directing and producing several Edgar Allen Poe adaptations often starring Vincent Price like *House of Usher* (1960), *Pit and the Pendulum* (1961) and *The Masque of the Red Death* (1964). Shot in vivid color with period costumes and sets, the 'Poe cycle' was something of an American answer to the popularity of the British Hammer horror movies that were enjoying huge success at the time. Never one to shy away from controversial subject matter, Corman also made several bold films that drew on hot topics of the decade including 1962's snapshot of racial tensions *The Intruder* (starring a young William Shatner), *The Wild Angels* (1966) and psychedelic acid odyssey *The Trip* (1967) all reflecting Corman's increasingly counter-culture tendencies.

As the 1970's approached, Corman grew disillusioned with the Hollywood establishment and became fed up with making small films for big studios who would often re-cut and edit them for release without his consent or knowledge. Desiring a break from the director's chair, and eager to have more of a hand in the distribution of films, he founded his own company; New World Pictures in 1970 which soon became the largest independent movie distribution company in the United States. As well as distributing the works of foreign masters like Fellini, Bergman and Kurosawa to American audiences, New World produced many of its own films, latching onto the seventies trends of blaxploitation and women in prison (WIP) pictures, including *The Big Doll House* (1971), *Women in Cages* (1971) and *T.N.T. Jackson* (1974).

The Arena (1974) starring Pam Grier was Corman's first foray into the sword and sandal type category made popular by the Italian peplum movies of the fifties and sixties, but it would be in the wake of *Conan the Barbarian*'s success that the first of several sword and sorcery movies would be produced by Corman.

The idea of doing such a movie was devised by Corman to utilize a new special effects lab he had formed to make *Battle Beyond the Stars* (1980); a *Star Wars* knock-off that was New World's most expensive movie to date. His choice of director was Jack Hill who had directed four Pam Grier-starring exploitation movies; *The Big Doll House* (1971) and *The Big Bird Cage* (1972) for New World Pictures as well as the popular *Coffy* (1973) and *Foxy Brown* (1974) for AIP.

Sorceress (1982)

Director: Jack Hill (as Brian Stuart)
Writer: Jim Wynorski

Jack Hill came up with the story for *Sorceress*; a tale of twin girls, raised in secret to save them from their evil father and cast Playboy Playmate twins Leigh and Lynette Harris as the sisters.

The movie opens with the evil sorcerer Traigon tracking down his wife who is hiding in the countryside. Traigon wants to sacrifice his firstborn to the goddess Kalghara. The trouble is, his wife has given birth to twins and refuses to tell him which was born first. Not even being horribly gouged by a claw-like implement will loosen her tongue. An elderly wizard called Krona appears to reprimand Traigon and, in the ensuing scuffle, the mother of the twins is able to impale her husband, cutting his tyrannical reign short before dying herself.

But Traigon has three lives and, Krona warns that he will return to finish his work. The twin girls must therefore be raised as boys to hide their identity. Krona magically gifts them with fighting skills and takes them to a nearby peasant couple to raise as their own.

Flash forward twenty years and the girls have grown up into the buxom Harris twins who are introduced in a gratuitous skinny-dipping scene. This is somewhat spoiled by the appearance of a bleating satyr who confuses the girls with what looks like a 'weapon between his legs'.

Mira and Mara, as the twins are now called, dress in boys' clothes (a disguise that apparently fools everybody) and return to their home to find it under attack by the minions of the returned Traigon. They put their martial skills to good use and see off the brigands but not before their adoptive mother and father are killed. Krona the wizard appears once more, looking decidedly older, and, with a bit of exposition, sets them on the path to revenge.

Along for the ride is a Viking called Baldar (looking like he stepped right out of a *Dungeons & Dragons* campaign), the aforementioned satyr, who we learn is called Pando, and a rather pretty-faced barbarian called Erlick. Highlights of the movie are a fight in the catacombs with some fairly effective zombies as well as one of the most inventive methods of execution ever put to film, involving a greased pole and a sharpened stake.

Needless to say, the movie doesn't take itself too seriously. Mira and Mara share a psychic bond similar to that shared by the titular characters of Alexandre Dumas's 1844 novel *The Corsican Brothers* meaning that they share physical sensations such as pain (and yes, orgasms). More humor is squeezed from the fact that the twins have grown up *thinking* they were boys and it is not until their ample breasts are pointed out by Erlick, that they concede that perhaps they are a little different to other boys ("See, Mira? Didn't I tell you there was something wrong?")

The theme of divine twins is a regular one in Indo-European mythology, particularly in Greek tradition. In fact, the costumes, goat-herding peasants and horny satyrs lend a definite Greek flavor to the fantasy world of *Sorceress* (*Clash of the Titans* was released the previous year to great success). This is despite Traigon's temple including a pair of giant Egyptian sphynxes apparently left over from some other movie.

Jack Hill shot the movie in Mexico and it was his last association with Roger Corman (and his last movie to date), something that can be put down to his experiences on the production. Hill was promised a decent budget for special effects as well as some known actors. Instead, the budget for special effects was far below expectations and the famous actors never materialized (Corman refused to pay for Hill's regular go-to man Sid Haig, whom Hill wanted for the role of Pando).

Once the film was out of Hill's hands, more cost-cutting practices were employed. Hill blames Corman for cutting the film down to its bare bones, removing an entire reel to save printing costs. Corman had the actors' voices dubbed by some of his office staff and even James Horner's score for *Battle Beyond the Stars* (his first feature-film score) was lifted wholesale and put to use in *Sorceress*; a trick Corman would repeat in several other movies. Hill was so displeased by the final result that he removed his name as director from the credits, 'Brian Stuart' being used instead.[16]

Trimmed-down and budgeted to within an inch of its life it may be, *Sorceress* was moderately successful, bringing enough return to New World Pictures to convince Corman to churn out more low-budget sword and sorcery flicks. That same year, he was approached by two Argentinian filmmakers, Héctor Olivera and Alejandro Sessa, with the proposition of making movies in Argentina.[17]

Olivera had co-founded Aries Cinematográfica Argentina in 1956 and was one of Argentina's most prolific writers, producers and directors. Alternating between commercial comedies and serious political films, Olivera recognized the need to make one type of movie to finance the other and he was keen to reach the U.S. market. Argentina had recently undergone a massive political change. The brutal military junta that had terrorized the country since 1976 collapsed, giving way to democracy and there was a push for foreign investment in movie co-productions.

For Corman, Argentina's cheap labor, materials and relaxed governmental regulations combined with a pre-existing, experienced film industry was an attractive proposition and he quickly went to work on the first of what would be ten movies he would make in Argentina. Seven of these would be sword and sorcery romps that recycled sets, costumes, actors and, occasionally, footage. They often had garish posters by the hand of Boris Vallejo that always promised something far better than the movies ever delivered.

Deathstalker (1983)

Director: James Sbardellati (as John Watson)
Writer: Howard R. Cohen (as Howard Cohen)

The first of Roger Corman's Argentinian movies was the most famous of his sword and sorcery efforts. James Sbardellati, who had been assistant director on two Corman-produced pictures; *Humanoids from the Deep* (1980) and *Battle Beyond the Stars* (1980), as well as first assistant director on *The Beastmaster* (1982) took to the director's chair for *Deathstalker*.

Rick Hill plays the title character of Deathstalker, a callous brute as far as barbarian swordsmen go, who is out for himself and himself only. "Heroes and fools are the same thing" he declares when the ousted King Tulak tries to persuade him to sneak into his castle and kill the wizard Munkar who has usurped him and kidnapped his daughter, Princess Codille (Playboy regular, Barbi Benton).

Munkar, a shape-shifting villain with a facial tattoo that inexplicably switches from one side of his head to the other throughout the movie, is holding a tournament to choose his successor. Naturally this draws every hero, fool and pig-headed brute (literally) from miles around to his castle for several days of wrestling, swordplay and debauchery.

There is also a quest to reunite the 'three powers of creation'. Two of them – the amulet and the chalice – are held by Munkar. The other – the sword – is safeguarded in a cave by a disfigured ape-man called

Salmaron. Directed to the cave by a witch, Deathstalker uses the sword to defeat an ogre and then lifts whatever curse Salmaron has been suffering under, reverting him to a middle-aged human who turns out to be the movie's comic relief character.

On the way to the tournament, they pick up the warrior Oghris played by Richard Brooker (fresh from playing Jason Voorhees in *Friday the 13th Part III*) and warrior woman Kaira (Lana Clarkson who would play several such characters for Corman in the years to come).

Meanwhile, in Munkar's suitably gothic castle, Princess Codille is placed in the wizard's harem and the tournament's contestants whoop it up in debauched scenes of feasting, fighting, raping and mudwrestling. In fact, the constant scenes of leering men having their way with screaming women makes the whole thing extra sleazy (and in this genre, that's saying a lot). The campy humor carried over from *Sorceress* jars somewhat with the icky-ness of *Deathstalker*'s shenanigans where even our 'hero' isn't above forcing himself on Princess Codille after foiling her assassination attempt. That the 'princess' is in fact one of Munkar's henchmen transformed into a doppelganger means that the whole thing was probably played for laughs but there is no denying that *Deathstalker* looks dated in more ways than one.

Deathstalker proved to be one of New World Pictures' highest-grossing movies ever, but by 1983, Roger Corman found himself running into financial difficulties. Even with its lucrative deal with Aries Cinematográfica Argentina, New World Pictures simply wasn't raking in enough cash anymore. One reason for this is that the drive-ins – the usual arena for Corman's pictures – were folding up and giving way to the home video market. Another was that there had been a large shift in the subject matter of the big film production companies. In previous decades, the exploitation and genre movies that Corman excelled at had been the product of small independent companies. But ever since *Jaws* (1975) and *Star Wars* (1977) the big shots had begun to make the same type of movies as the independent studios, naturally injecting large amounts of financial backing with which smaller companies simply could not compete. In 1983, Corman cut a deal with a triumvirate of lawyers and sold New World Pictures for 16.5 million.

Corman retained the rights to his back catalogue of movies and kept most of his production staff, leaving the new owners of New World Pictures with distribution (a side of the business Corman had never particularly liked). The deal was that New World Pictures would distribute Corman's films while he would focus on production. The deal fell apart when New World Pictures refused to distribute his movies and, after some legal wrangling resulting in a settlement, Corman found himself lumbered with distributing his own movies once again.

Corman had already founded a new production company called Millennium which quickly changed its name to New Horizons. In 1985 he formed Concorde as its distribution arm, eventually merging the two as Concorde-New Horizons. He found himself perfectly placed to take advantage of the burgeoning home video market. Many of his new movies still appeared in theatres but the profitability of low-budget genre movies on video made theatrical releases little more than advertising in order to secure video profits.

The key to profitability was volume, and Concorde-New Horizons increased production dramatically. Until then, Corman had always overseen every production of his from start to finish but the drastic increase of movies made per year meant that he could no longer give them the same attention as he used to. This resulted in a drop in quality in many of the movies he produced but, with so many hitting the racks of video stores worldwide, Concorde-New Horizons still drew a hefty profit.[18]

The Warrior and the Sorceress (1984)

Director: John C. Broderick (as John Broderick)
Writer: John C. Broderick (as John Broderick)
William Stout (story)

David Carradine starred in Roger Corman's next sword and sorcery adventure as the wandering swordsman Kain (presumably an intentional reference to his character 'Caine' from the TV series *Kung Fu*). Roaming the deserts of a distant planet (lit by two suns ala *Star Wars*), Kain approaches a dusty settlement called Yamatar where two rival warlords fight for control of the village's only well. One of them is Bal Caz (Guillermo Marín); a rotund letch who spends most of his time lolling on cushions with his pet lizard surrounded by naked ladies. The other is Zeg (Luke Askew), a decidedly more warrior-like figure who is holding a mysterious woman captive (played by Argentine actress Maria Socas).

Kain initially sides with Bal Caz after slaying some of Zeg's men guarding the well. Overhearing his new employer's plans to have him killed once he has outlived his usefulness, Kain ditches Bal Caz at a crucial moment, leaving the two warlords to fight it out in the village streets.

A troupe of travelling slavers have arrived to sell their wares and Bal Caz poisons the water Zeg has sold them in an effort to frame him. Kain sells this information to Zeg and joins his company (who like to entertain themselves by ogling a four-breasted dancing girl).

Now in Zeg's employ, Kain is able to learn more about the mysterious woman Zeg has under lock and key. Her name is Naja and is presumably the sorceress of the title for she holds the ability to re-forge the Sacred Sword of Yura which Zeg is demanding of her. As well as playing the two gangs against each other, Kain makes it his business to rescue Naja and reunite her with her father.

If the basic plot sounds familiar, you're not wrong. It's yet another remake of Akira Kurosawa's 1961 samurai classic *Yojimbo* (which in turn, drew influence from Dashiell Hammett's 1929 pulp novel *Red Harvest*). Like *A Fistful of Dollars* (1964) before it, *The Warrior and the Sorceress* covers the same story beats as *Yojimbo*; that of a lone drifter entering a town controlled by two warring factions. Playing one off against the other, the drifter makes a fortune, reunites a kidnapped lady with her loved one and departs, leaving a trail of corpses in his wake. The formula would be reworked again in 1996's *Last Man Standing* which returned the versatile tale to its prohibition era roots.

Grey-haired and stringy, David Carradine presents an unlikely hero for a sword and sorcery flick. He was already a Corman alumni, having previously appeared in *Boxcar Bertha* (1972) and *Death Race 2000* (1975). He may not look the part, but his character is a good example of sword and sorcery's self-serving antiheroes and the plot involving corrupt rulers of seedy locales is a common trope of the genre.

Originally titled 'Kane of the Dark Planet'[19], *The Warrior and the Sorceress* is an interesting attempt at sword and planet but there is little follow up on the concept. The planet has two suns but that's about all that distinguishes it from any other generic fantasy setting. There are no ray guns or other identifiers of futuristic technology. There are some throwaway references to the collapse of a central government and Kain seems to belong to a disbanded holy order so we seem to be dealing with a post-apocalyptic scenario, but it is never expanded on.

Wizards of the Lost Kingdom (1985)

Director: Héctor Olivera
Writer: Ed Naha (as Tom Edwards)

While the words 'Roger Corman' and 'family movie' in the same sentence may sound like a cause for concern, *Wizards of the Lost Kingdom* was likely an attempt to cash in on the success of the previous year's kids fantasy hit *The NeverEnding Story* (1984). Along with *Dragonslayer* (1981) and *The Dark Crystal* (1982) it was clear that that there was a market for family-orientated fantasy movies.

The film's prologue consists entirely of recycled footage from *Sorceress* and *Deathstalker* (the bits without blood or nudity) with James Horner's *Battle Beyond the Stars* score put to use once again. We find ourselves in the kingdom of Axeholme where King Tylor (Augusto Laretta who played Salmaron in *Deathstalker*) is usurped by the evil wizard Shurka (Thom Christopher). Aiding in the coup is Tylor's queen Udea (Barbara Stock) who is also Shurka's lover, although it quickly becomes apparent that Shurka is intending to trade her in for a younger model as he begins to leer at her teenage daughter, Princess Aura (Dolores Michaels).

After slaying the king, Shurka comes for the court wizard Wulfrick (Edgardo Moreira), who passes his magic ring to his son Simon (Vidal Peterson). Simon and his companion, Gulfax (a tall, hairy white creature that echoes *Star Wars*'s Chewbacca), are whisked away by Wulfrick's magic before they can fall into Shurka's hands but the magic ring tumbles from Simon's hand as he departs. Stranded in a forest with Shurka's soldiers looking for him (and his magic ring), Simon sets out on a quest for vengeance and to free his friend, Princess Aura.

Fortunately, Simon and Gulfax meet wandering swordsman, Kor the Conqueror (Bo Svensen), who becomes something of a guide and mentor to young Simon. The trio have various adventures along the way including an encounter with a shapeshifting forest sorceress (Maria Socas from *The Warrior and the Sorceress*) who drugs Simon resulting in a dream sequence cobbled together from yet more footage from *Sorceress*. Although, as the footage is from *Sorceress*'s climax, it is wholly without context and confuses rather than clarifies the proceedings.

Héctor Olivera of Aries Cinematográfica Argentina directed this one himself and it's a colorful movie with lots of bright costumes and a castle set that looks more like it was made for a theme park than a movie. Some high points involve a spot of necromancy on Simon's part that results in four rather good zombie warriors rising from their graves and a journey through a series of caves where our heroes are assailed by floating specters.

Wizards of the Lost Kingdom, with its family friendly tone and 'save the kingdom' plot doesn't scream sword and sorcery, but it is an example of Roger Corman bending the genre to capitalize on other trends. His next few movies would return to the gory, nudity-filled adult fantasy he is more commonly known for.

Barbarian Queen (1985)

Director: Héctor Olivera
Writer: Howard R. Cohen

Héctor Olivera's second movie for Corman in the same year was a definite return to a more adult tone. Bearing many similarities to *Hundra* (1983) and the then-in-production *Red Sonja* (1985), *Barbarian Queen*'s finest asset by far is the athletic and energetic Lana Clarkson.

Born in 1962, Long Beach, California, Clarkson worked as a model in the late seventies before landing bit parts in sitcoms such as *Three's Company* and *The Jeffersons* as well as a walk-on role in *Scarface* (1983) along with fellow *Barbarian Queen* star Katt Shea (who would go on to direct four movies for Corman). Following her role as the warrior woman Kaira in *Deathstalker*, Corman decided that Clarkson could carry a film by herself and cast her as Amethea, the titular Barbarian Queen.

Queen Amethea is about to celebrate her wedding to the handsome Argan (Frank Zagarino). The festivities are cut short by attacking raiders who slaughter almost everyone and enslave the rest, including Amethea's little sister, Taramis.

Amethea survives along with two of her friends; Estrild (Katt Shea) and Tiniara (Susana Traverso). Taking a boat downriver, the trio rescue a traumatized Taramis from a group of the raiders who are hanging out at a riverside shack, drinking and dicing. Amathea then swears vengeance in the movie's most memorable line; "I'll be no man's slave and no man's whore, and if I can't kill them all, by the gods they'll know I've tried."

Their path to vengeance leads them to a group of rebels who are fighting against the cruel tyrant Arrakur (Armando Capo who played the masked slaver Burgo in *The Warrior and the Sorceress*). It was Arrakur who led the assault against Amethea's village and he currently rules from a nearby city. The only one who can lead them into the city is the waifish Dariac (Andrea Scriven) who sneaks them beneath the city gates to some catacombs where her father and the rest of the rebels are hiding. Nevertheless, the rebels aren't too keen for Amethea and her friends to start stirring up trouble, fearing that their burgeoning rebellion isn't ready for the heat that would bring.

While snooping around the city's marketplace, Amethea learns that Argan and a few other men from her village are alive and enslaved as gladiators. Taramis wanders off and Estrild stumbles through the marketplace looking for her and gets herself captured. Taramis spots Arrakur and willingly goes with him. Whether this is a plan to get close to him and kill him or if her trauma has resulted in some sort of Stockholm syndrome isn't quite explained.

Amethea and Tiniara desperately try to rescue Estrild but end up captured too. After some unsavory rape and torture scenes, it is up to Amethea to escape and enlist both rebels and gladiators in the final battle that will bring about Arrakur's downfall.

Barbarian Queen dials down on the fantasy and its total lack of anything resembling sorcery makes it more of a sword and sandal flick akin to Corman's 1974 production, *The Arena*. Its short running time (72 minutes) is likely due to it not recycling any footage from previous movies (something of a rarity for a Corman production).

Being an exploitation movie, the notion of strong, independent women overcoming a patriarchal tyranny is undermined by plenty of gratuitous rape scenes, nudity aplenty and a lengthy scene where Amethea is stripped and tied to a rack while a clawed hand gropes her bare breasts. Despite quite literally crushing her captor's manhood in one of the most unique methods of escape ever put to film, there is no ambiguity as to who the target audience is here, and it isn't feminists.

Amazons (1986)

Director: Alejandro Sessa (as Alex Sessa)
Writer: Charles Saunders

With the success of the previous year's *Barbarian Queen*, a second variation on the warrior woman formula was quickly put into production and, rather unusually, Corman turned to an existing literary source.

Imaro creator Charles R. Saunders had written the short story *Agbewe's Sword* for the 1979 anthology *Amazons!* published by Daw and edited by Jessica Amanda Salmonson. Significant for featuring solely female protagonists and written primarily by female authors, the anthology went on to win the 1980 World Fantasy Award for Best Anthology.

As with his Imaro stories, *Agbewe's Sword* is set in a fantasy world inspired by the culture and history of West Africa. Heroine Dossouye is part of the *ahosi*, an elite female fighting force who are brides of the tribe's 'Leopard King'. After being defeated by a neighboring tribe who summon lightning to attack them, Dossouye receives a vision from Agbewe, the spider goddess, and sets out to find the titular sword that can defeat their enemies. But so too does, Nyima, commander of the ahosi who despises Dossouye with a passion.

Saunders adapted the screenplay himself although it probably wasn't his idea to ditch the pseudo-African setting for a generic fantasy world peopled almost entirely with white characters. Rather than seeing this as a classic case of whitewashing, it may be more charitable to assume that it was a result of the movie being filmed in Argentina with local talent providing a cheaper alternative to flying in black actors.

The main character in *Amazons* is Dyala, played by Mindi Miller (credited as Windsor Taylor Randolph); a member of the elite bikini-clad warrior women of the Emerald Queen. After an attack by the wicked sorcerer Kalungo (Joseph Whipp) who can zap people with lightning, Dyala is selected to journey across the Cursed Lands in search of the legendary Sword of Azundati.

Tashinge (Danitza Kingsley), captain of the queen's guard, sends her own daughter, Tashi (Penelope Reed) with Dyala to protect her. But she has an ulterior motive born of a family feud. Dyala's mother and Tashinge once fought over a man resulting in Tashinge losing a hand. She's keen for vengeance and instructs her daughter to do away with Dyala once they have the sword.

Further treachery is revealed when Tashinge visits Kalungo in his lair and promises to ensure that the sword will never be used against him. Surmising that if Tashinge can betray her own people, then she might betray him too, Kalungo dispatches his own agent, Akam (who can shapeshift into a lion), to kill Dyala and Tashi once they have found the sword and bring it to him.

Meanwhile, our bethonged beauties have taken a break from their journey for a quick skinny dip and are rudely interrupted by a group of leering men. Akam in her lion form helps chase off the scoundrels and our heroines are on their way once more.

An episodic series of scrapes ensue, involving a fight with a big snake and capture by a murderous cult. Dyala and Tashi eventually come across an old prophetess in her hut who guides them on the final stage of their journey. The Sword of Azundati lies in the 'shining cave' but she cryptically warns them that three will enter but only one will leave.

The plot with its rivalries and backstabbing is a lot more intricate than Corman's other barbarian movies, something that can probably be credited to having an accomplished writer like Saunders onboard. Héctor Olivera took a back seat as producer this time with Alejandro Sessa taking the first of what would be only two turns in the director's chair.

Stormquest (1987)

Director: Alejandro Sessa (as Alex Sessa)
Writer: Charles Saunders

Alejandro Sessa and Charles R. Saunders immediately collaborated on a second venture into the world of scantily clad warrior women. This time, Sessa came up with the story and Saunders adapted it.

The movie starts with a lengthy prologue that tells us nothing about plot or character as it is a series of disjointed scenes from the movie we are about to see entirely without context or voiceover. We then find ourselves in the kingdom of Kimbia which is all female, having overthrown the old patriarchy. The only contact they have with men from other tribes is to "get their seed and return their male children to them."

Three women are on trial. Tani (Monica Gonzaga) is accused of stealing from the treasury. Asha (Christina Whitaker) has committed the sin of loving a man and Kinya (Dudzie Mkhize) has released the goddess Zimbi (who resides in the form of a lioness) into the wild. The high judge sentences the trio to death by drowning at the Thunder Falls which will wash them away from Kimbia. First, they are dealt twenty lashes apiece "for the edification of the people."

Meanwhile, the neighboring kingdom of Ishtan is having similar ideas to Kimbia. It is ruled by the 'Stormqueen' (Linda Lutz), a rotund sadist who dresses like Ming the Merciless and giggles manically as she steps on the groins of her male slaves to comedic 'crunching' sounds. All men in Ishtan are divided in 'studs' and 'drones' representing their basic functions. There is however, some sort of men's liberation movement led by Zar (Brent Huff) who, with a bunch of fellow revolutionaries, escapes Ishtan and head for the Thunder Falls.

There, they stumble across the imminent executions and rescue the three women. Asha, Tani and Kinya quickly decide that joining in Ishtan's revolution is preferable to sticking around in Kimbia.

The band of rebels are attacked by the Stormqueen's forces and Tani switches sides, agreeing to help the Stormqueen hunt down the rebels and their new allies. Zar is captured and tied up in the Stormqueen's bedchamber where, accompanied by the giggling of her pet snake, the tyrant reveals that she isn't actually a woman at all.

Kinya returns to Kimbia and, with the help of the lion goddess, overthrows the high judge while Asha rescues Zar and the other prisoners from the 'death chase' which consists of being pursued through a forest by masked slaves in bondage gear.

Released directly to home video in the U.S. in 1988, *Stormquest*, with its giggling snakes and fetishistic undertones, is the most bizarre and obscure entry in Corman's sword and sorcery output.

Deathstalker II: Duel of the Titans (1987)

Director: Jim Wynorski

Writer: Jim Wynorski (story), Neil Ruttenberg (screenplay), R.J. Robertson (additional dialogue)

Those well-used sets in Argentina were beginning to fall apart by 1987 but Corman was determined to wring one more movie out of them, this time with Jim Wynorski at the helm; a man who would go on to have a long association with Corman and a prolific career in exploitation movies.

Wynorski had just directed the horror comedy *Chopping Mall* (1986) for Corman's wife, Julie Corman, who had her own production company named Trinity Pictures. Unimpressed by the original script written by Neil Ruttenberg, Wynorski threw it out and wrote a more lightweight one with *Chopping Mall* star John Terlesky.[20] Terlesky was cast as Deathstalker and Wynorski's then-girlfriend (and Penthouse Pet of the Month) Monique Gabrielle starred as the hero's love interest.

The movie opens with a James Bond-ish prologue that has Deathstalker steal a gemstone from the villain Sultana (Toni Naples) who is none too pleased, declaring "I'll have my revenge. And Deathstalker too!" This campy reference to the movie's very title segues into the funky synth-pop of the credits sequence, setting the tone for the whole movie. To say that it doesn't take itself too seriously is an understatement.

The waifish Reena (Monique Gabrielle) is kicked out of a tavern while claiming that she is really a princess. Deathstalker is on hand to stop the rough treatment and, a rousing barfight and a moonlit horse chase later, our main characters rest up in Reena's hovel for some soup and a spot of exposition.

Reena is a seer and gives Deathstalker a free reading. There is a princess, she explains, held captive by Jarek, the evil sorcerer ("Is there any other kind" Deathstalker muses). Defeat the sorcerer and rescue the princess is the order of the day, a feat that, Reena affirms, will get Deathstalker's name into the legends "right up there with Conan."

Cut to the villain's castle where Jarek, the rather suave sorcerer (John Lazar), is honing his sword skills while a familiar-looking princess looks on. 'Evie' as we are told her name is, was created by Jarek from the soul of the original princess who has now escaped. Jarek is also in league with Sultana, the evil woman from the prologue who has a bone to pick with Deathstalker and agrees to capture the runaway princess if she is able to do as she pleases with our barbarian hero.

Deathstalker and Reena stop to rob a crypt and, while Reena is being chased around outside by the newly-risen dead, Deathstalker is trapped inside and narrowly escapes being crushed by a spiked wall – "The old crushing wall routine, huh?" he quips.

More dastardliness is revealed back at Jerak's castle. Evie, it appears, is having occasionally vanishing fits, something to do with imperfections in Jarek's formula when he cloned her. She is also a vampire, revealed by her feeding on a hapless peasant boy whose screaming face she adds to her collection on her bed's headboard. This particular headboard will look familiar to anyone who's been paying attention to Corman's fantasy romps, as it appeared in the lairs of several other villains.

A group of women led by Maria Socas (now a veteran of these flicks) wearing what appear to be costumes left over from *Amazons* and *Stormquest*, capture Reena and Deathstalker. Their suspicions that Reena is in fact 'Evie the demon princess' who burns their crops and steals their men are quickly dismissed but the amazons have also heard of Deathstalker, in particular his womanizing ways. Thoroughly unimpressed, they put Deathstalker on trial for his 'crimes against womanhood'.

The trial takes the form of a fight to the death against a large, redheaded woman (professional wrestler Dee Boher using her ring name 'Queen Kong') that takes place in a roped wrestling ring complete with bikinied women holding scorecards and a musical cue that rips off the *Rocky* theme. Naturally Deathstalker wins but, despite it being declared a fight to the death, refuses to kill his opponent. This seems to impress Maria Soca's amazon queen who decides to marry Deathstalker. He splits, leaving the queen looking most irate in her wedding gown; "Aw, shit!" she pouts.

There is a sense that Jim Wynorski and co. really had a blast with this one. There's even a mid-credits blooper reel. Gone are the nasty rape scenes of the first Deathstalker; instead there are wisecracks and self-referential humor that makes *Deathstalker II* almost come off as a parody of the first movie. As the low box-office draw of *Red Sonja* indicated that the genre had started to grow a little stale, the slapstick fight scenes, nods to genre clichés and the "is that your sword or are you just happy to see me?" one-liners of

Deathstalker II showed that, by 1987, even Corman's low-budget knockoffs had started to poke fun at themselves.

Deathstalker and the Warriors from Hell (1988)

Director: Alfonso Corona
Writer: Howard R. Cohen (as Howard Cohen)

Deathstalker II was the last of Roger Corman's run of movies to be shot in Argentina but, although his relationship with Aries Cinematográfica Argentina was over, that didn't mean he was done with sword and sorcery movies or even the Deathstalker franchise.

Back to shooting in Mexico, Corman turned the script for a third installment over to Howard R. Cohen who had written the first *Deathstalker* as well as *Barbarian Queen*. *Deathstalker and the Warriors from Hell* featured yet another new face as the title character in the form of John Allen Nelson who matched neither the wisecracking antics of John Terlesky or the brutish savagery of Rick Hill.

The movie begins with a festival involving the usual flutey music, soothsaying and wrestling matches. A hooded woman arrives in search of the wizard, Nicias, who is amusing the crowd with tarot readings and magic tricks. This woman is Princess Carissa (Carla Sands who would go on to become the U.S. ambassador to Denmark of all things) and she has one half of a magic stone in her possession. Black-clad riders suddenly attack the festival looking for the wizard (and presumably the stone too). Fortunately, Deathstalker is on hand and the wizard instructs him to look after the princess before teleporting himself to safety.

Deathstalker and Carissa gallop away and she fills him in on the legend of the secret city of Arendor, which is home to Nicias the wizard and filled with riches. Those pesky black riders catch up with them and murder Carissa. With her dying breath, she sets Deathstalker up on his quest; reunite two halves of a magic stone to reveal the secret city. She gives him her half and tells him that a powerful warlord in the Southland has the other.

We are then introduced to the powerful warlord in question and it's Thom Christopher on villain duties again after his turn in *Wizards of the Lost Kingdom* (although this time sporting some very unfortunate fashion choices). His name is Troxartes and he wants the other half of the stone, not so he can plunder the secret city's riches, but apparently the stones of Arendor are a source of great magic in themselves.

On his way to the Southland, Deathstalker comes across a princess that is the spitting image of Carissa (because she is also played by Carla Sands). Troxartes's soldiers turn up once again and Deathstalker demands that the princess conceal him on pain of her life (and he gets in a quick grope for good measure, indicating that perhaps the old Deathstalker is with us after all). After evading capture, Deathstalker then gets busted trying to steal a horse from warrior woman Marinda (Claudia Inchaurregui) and her mother who like eating potatoes ("Potatoes are what we eat" being one of the movie's more memorable lines). Deathstalker offers to pay for a night's lodging and then has his wicked way with Marinda in the night.

Marinda shows promise as a female companion in the Lana Clarkson mold but, unfortunately, Deathstalker ditches her and heads for the forest where he hooks up with the spoiled princess he assaulted earlier. She turns out to be Princess Elizena, the twin sister of Carissa, and was on her way to marry Troxartes until Deathstalker turned up and ruined everything. All her bodyguards were killed by Troxartes's men during Deathstalker's escape and now she's all alone. Not liking Deathstalker much, she wanders off and is picked up by her groom to be. Now Deathstalker has a princess to rescue as well as a gem to steal.

Back at Troxartes's castle (a reused shot from Corman's 1963 movie *The Raven*), Troxartes raises the dead against Deathstalker while wearing a very fetching pink fur robe accompanied by some reused shots from *Wizards of the Lost Kingdom*. These are presumably the titular 'warriors from Hell' but they are hardly important enough to warrant being part of the movie's title.

A lackluster hero going from one repetitive set piece to the next before eventually confronting a thoroughly bland villain makes this the least popular of the Deathstalker series. Following neither the comedic route of its predecessor nor the sleazy adult tone of the first Deathstalker, *Deathstalker III* is a bit like its lead; passable but unremarkable and ultimately forgettable.

Wizards of the Lost Kingdom II (1989)

Director: Charles B. Griffith
Writer: Charles B. Griffith, Lance Smith

The success of *Wizards of the Lost Kingdom* on home video encouraged Roger Corman to take another crack at a family friendly fantasy movie. Writer Charles B. Griffith, who had lent a dark comedic flair to several of Corman's early productions such as *A Bucket of Blood* (1959) and *The Little Shop of Horrors* (1960), headed to Mexico to shoot what is essentially a few additional scenes to connect footage nabbed from other movies.

Wizards of the Lost Kingdom II is a sequel in name only, sharing neither plot nor characters with its predecessor. After a prologue that may as well be a greatest hits reel of Corman's previous sword and sorcery flicks, it opens with the bumbling old wizard Caedmon emerging from his cave (Mel Welles, who had played the hapless shop owner in *The Little Shop of Horrors*). Contacted by his superior wizard, Vanir (Wayne Grace), Caedmon is dispatched on his quest. The three powers of creation have been divided by three evil wizards; Loki, Donar and Zarz. Caedmon must seek out the one whose pure heart can reunite these three powers.

Without further ado, Caedmon tracks down a boy called Tyor (Robert Jayne) whom he identifies as the youth he is looking for by a birthmark in his armpit. We also learn that the three forces of creation are a chalice, a sword and an amulet; exactly as they are in

Deathstalker. A nice hint at a shared universe or another sign that truly everything is recyclable in these movies?

During a brief stop in a tavern, Caedmon tries to recruit the innkeeper who is known only as 'the Dark One' and played by David Carradine. His identical costume to his character in *The Sword and the Sorceress* is an obvious attempt to retain continuity with the liberal reuse of footage from that movie.

Having three MacGuffins held by three villains provides an easy three act plot. First Caedmon and Tyor rescue muscular hero Erman from Loki's castle and steal the amulet. Then it's on to MacGuffin number two; the sword, held by Donar (Sid Haig in a rather feathery outfit).

En route, Caedmon and Tyor cross paths with a familiar blonde warrior woman played by Lana Clarkson. The slight spelling difference suggests that the Amathea of this movie is not the 'Amethea' Clarkson played in *Barbarian Queen* and it would have been a strange move to link this bloodless adventure with Clarkson's decidedly more adult caper.

Amathea leads them into the city with the aim of rescuing some of her warriors whom Donar is using as gladiators. What follows constitutes nearly an entire scene plucked from *Barbarian Queen* reinforcing the notion that just about everything about this plot was contrived to get away with shooting the bare minimum of new footage possible.

Tyor steals the magic sword and hands it over to Amathea who promises that she and her warriors will follow him into battle. We then get a good portion of the climactic battle from *Barbarian Queen* before Tyor confronts Donar who promptly vanishes in a puff of feathers.

The final villain is Zarz played by Henry Brandon in his last film role (he would die the following year). The gang pick up David Carradine before advancing on Zarz's castle and we are treated to a number of scenes from *The Warrior and the Sorceress* before Zarz and Donar receive their comeuppance and peace is restored throughout the kingdom.

Certainly humorous, but not quite the level of tongue-in-cheek parody seen in *Deathstalker II*, *Wizards of the Lost Kingdom II* would have been a considerably short movie were it not for the extensive recycling of work already paid for and surely ranks among Corman's most audacious penny-pinching ventures.

Barbarian Queen II: The Empress Strikes Back (1990)

Director: Joe Finley

Writer: Howard R. Cohen (screenplay), Lance Smith (screenplay and story)

A sequel in only the loosest sense of the term, the second Barbarian Queen trades the loincloths and sandals of its predecessor for a pseudo-medieval setting more suited to Robin Hood than Conan the Barbarian. Instead of the fierce warrior woman, Amethea, Lana Clarkson plays 'Athalia'; a sheltered princess who rails against being made to dress like a lady.

Upon the death of her father in battle, Athalia is cast into the dungeons by the usurper Ankaris (Alejandro Bracho). There is a magic scepter held in the castle, the power of which is key to ruling the kingdom. The scepter is useless without knowing the magic words and these were entrusted to Athalia by her late father. Naturally, Ankaris wants to worm them out of her.

Aided by Ankaris's own daughter, Tamis (Cecilia Tijerina), Athalia escapes her cell and tries to steal the scepter. But it was all a ruse on the part of the bratty Tamis to get her to say the magic words. Athalia is recaptured and sentenced to death. She escapes once more and gallops away on a stolen horse.

She finds allies in a tribe of forest-dwelling warrior women. After being sneered at for her fine clothes, Athalia proves herself in a topless mud wrestle and is accepted as one of the gals. Now clad in leather bikini and miniskirt, Athalia rises to the top of the tribe and rallies them against Ankaris's forces.

During a raid on a slave caravan, they capture Ankaris's top henchman Hofrax (Roger Cudney), as well as Athalia's handsome ex-flame Aurion (Greg Wrangler) who is now due to marry the obnoxious Tamis. Aurion and Athalia take the chance to hook up once more but it's kept hush-hush as Aurion is sent back to the castle with Hofrax.

Then, taking a leaf from many a Robin Hood movie, Ankaris devises a public hanging of innocents to draw the outlaws into his trap. Disguised as nuns, Athalia and her friends get close enough to the prisoners to stage a rescue. It all goes to plan until Athalia is captured. Back in the dungeons, she finds herself tied to a rack and stripped to the waist in a scene remarkably similar to the one in the first movie, although surprisingly for a Corman movie, it's not recycled footage. Aurion rescues her and finally throws in his lot with the outlaws, joining in the third act assault on the castle.

Despite being shot in 1988, *Barbarian Queen II* was kept in limbo until a Japanese VHS release in 1990. The rest of the world had to wait until 1992 to catch up on the latest Lana Clarkson adventure. The *Barbarian Queen* movies, along with her roles in *Deathstalker* and *Wizards of the Lost Kingdom II*, cemented Clarkson's reputation as a cult b-movie screen queen of the eighties and Corman himself has fondly referred to her as 'the original Xena Warrior Princess'.

Sadly, Clarkson's cinematic career took something of a dive in the nineties with mostly TV roles and commercials being thrown her way. To make ends meet, she took a part-time job as a hostess at the House of Blues in Los Angeles. In the early hours of February 2nd, 2003, she went home with renowned record producer Phil Spector to his Alhambra mansion. Not long after, Spector's driver made an emergency call, reporting a gunshot. Police arrived and found Clarkson's body slumped in a chair with a gunshot wound to the mouth. Two trials followed, resulting in Spector being sentenced to nineteen years to life for her murder.

Deathstalker IV: Match of Titans (1991)

Director: Howard R. Cohen

Writer: Howard R. Cohen, Beverly Gray (story editor)

It would be remiss not to cover the final installment in the Deathstalker saga despite it being filmed in late 1990 and not making its way to home video until the following year. Howard R. Cohen (who had written the first and third Deathstalkers as well as both Barbarian Queens) headed to Bulgaria to shoot what is arguably the most polished in the series.

As is the norm by now, we are given a prologue consisting of reused footage which culminates in a shot from the first *Deathstalker* featuring Rick Hill chopping up mutants. Which was deliberate as Rick Hill is back for this final installment in the franchise.

He starts off (in a much better wig this time) by rescuing a young woman from some lion men. He escorts her to her village which just happens to be his own destination. He's looking for his friend Aldilar (Stancho Stanchev) with whom he has had some adventures but "things got a little confusing. He wound up with my sword and I with his." Deathstalker wants his sword back but it is never clear if this is more important to him than rescuing his old comrade.

Aldilar is nowhere to be found so Deathstalker continues on his journey, coming across a fellow warrior called Vaniat (Brett Baxter Clark). Vaniat is training for an upcoming tournament held by evil sorceress Kana (Michelle Moffett) whose warriors have been tearing up the countryside of late. Vaniat's training routine consists of night-time pushups and avoiding chasing women as it "saps your vital juices". Continuing together, Deathstalker and Vaniat rescue warrior woman Dionara (Maria Ford) from some uglies and then it's on to the tournament at Kana's castle.

Titillating shenanigans ensue on the first night for, just as Deathstalker and Dionara are getting to know each other, Kana orders all the female warriors to the great hall while she slips into Deathstalker's chamber. She's after men and strong ones at that, although her motives appear to be something other than carnal.

The tournament proceeds and Deathstalker cottons on to Kana's plan. She's plucking the best of the tournament fighters and turning them into her private army of stone warriors. How she manages this is left vague although it seems to involve drugged wine, sex and sorcery. Deathstalker also spots his old sword in Kana's possession and surmises that his friend Aldilar came to a sticky end at her hands. Working together, Deathstalker, Dionara and Vaniat come up with a scheme to foil Kana's dastardly plans.

Deathstalker IV: Match of the Titans marked the end of Roger Corman's foray into sword and sorcery, at least as far as the genre boom of the 1980s was concerned. There had been plans for a third *Barbarian Queen* movie (titled *Barbarian Queen III: Revenge of the She-King*) to be shot in Bulgaria directly following *Deathstalker IV* but the movie never materialized.[21] By the early nineties, the market had been truly saturated and other trends had emerged that were worth capitalizing on. The impending success of *Jurassic Park*

(1993) prompted Corman to beat it to the theatre by one month with *Carnosaur* (1993); a dino romp that spawned two sequels, but the nature of the industry had also changed and Corman's tactic of relying on unknown directors willing to work cheap was becoming more difficult.

The Sundance Film Festival – the largest independent film festival in the United States – became a route for success in the early nineties for young directors like Quentin Tarantino and Steven Soderbergh. By providing exposure for independent movies, Sundance presented a real alternative for up and coming directors who, a decade previously, may have found themselves making their bones by churning out a few Corman movies.[22]

SPAGHETTI SWORD AND SORCERY – THE ITALIAN CONNECTION

"When a man meets a man, you never know which one will die. But when an animal meets a man, it's always the animal that dies. I'm on the animals' side." - Mace, *Conquest* (1983)

One country that can always be counted on to churn out their own answer to popular American trends is Italy and it was no different in the bloody wake of *Conan the Barbarian.* The Italian film industry, once considered a respectable arena for auteurs and art-film directors, was in trouble by the dawn of the 1980s. In the preceding decades, the Italian art film had become increasingly separated from more low-budget genre offerings such as the spaghetti western and the slew of gruesome horror films produced in the 1970s. But before these cheap subgenres became Italian cinema's most famous export, a group of films known as 'pepla' grew in popularity and can be seen as the ancestral genre to the sword and sorcery movie of the 1980s.

Pepla (singular; peplum), are named after an over-the-shoulder article of clothing worn in ancient Greece as the movies themselves typically feature Greco-Roman mythology, biblical or historical subject matter. A subgenre of the sword and sandal movie, the genre occasionally featured magic and monsters, although most eschewed the supernatural. Pepla often dealt with evil priests, wicked usurpers and captured princesses and came to prominence in the late fifties in the wake of *Le Fatiche di Ercole* (1957) starring American bodybuilder Steve Reeves. Released as *Hercules* in the U.S., the film was hugely popular and kick-started a trend in Italian cinema. A further eighteen Hercules movies were made with various muscular actors playing the role.

As well as using other characters from mythology such as Samson and Goliath, Italian filmmakers were keen to dig up other muscular heroes and an original character from Italy's silent period was revived. Maciste, who had first appeared as a sidekick in *Cabiria* (1914), had been the hero of over twenty silent movies that had him appearing everywhere from the Ice Age to the 16th century. The return of Maciste in the era of sound and color began with 1960's *Maciste nella Valle dei Re* (*Son of Samson*) which spawned a further twenty-five movies. Another Hercules clone was Ursus (originally a character in Henryk Sienkiewicz's 1895 novel *Quo Vadis* and its film adaptations) who spawned a nine-movie series.

As the names of Maciste and Ursus were largely unfamiliar to American audiences, they were often given more recognizable names like Hercules and Samson when they were dubbed and marketed for release in the U.S. In addition, the 1960s TV series *Sons of Hercules* repackaged thirteen peplum movies with a standardized theme song and attempted to connect them all to the famous Greek demigod.

The era of the peplum movie, although prolific, was short-lived. Sergio Leone's *Per un Pugno di Dollari* (*A Fistful of Dollars*) was released in 1964 to tremendous success and caused many Italian filmmakers to trade in their swords and loincloths for spurs and six-shooters. Originally a derogatory term for Italian-made westerns, the 'spaghetti western' rejuvenated a genre that had largely fizzled in the U.S. due to tough competition from television. The spaghetti western trod similar ground to the sword and sorcery movie, especially the template of a lone fighter entering a dusty village and setting things to rights in a short, down and dirty street-level narrative.

Magic, monsters and swordplay remained notably absent from Italian cinema for close to two decades as the spaghetti western rolled on into the seventies and descended into comedy and self-parody. Other genres received more attention such as the 'giallo' film. Giallo (meaning 'yellow') originally referred to cheap mystery paperbacks with yellow covers popular in Italy's wartime period (much like the French *Série noire* publishing imprint that lent its name to the Film Noir movement). By the 1960s, the term giallo had also encompassed film, albeit in a less defined way. Giallo films ranged from psychological thrillers to horror-slashers by directors like Dario Argento and Lucio Fulci and, as the seventies wore on, grew more and more gory and shocking. It was at this time that Italian horror gained bloody notoriety with 'Mondo films'; pseudo-documentaries intended to shock and disturb that focused on cannibalism and gruesome tribal rites. These movies bled out onto the home video market amid much controversy and became staples of what an appalled British National Viewers' and Listeners' Association (NVLA) dubbed 'video nasties'.

After the success of the 1981 French movie *La guerre du feu* (Quest for Fire), more caveman movies started to pop up. They were cheap to make and shared some common ground with the sword and sorcery genre. With the addition of some magic and the occasional rubber monster, you have a low-budget sword and sorcery flick that can be marketed as a Conan clone.

By the 1980s, the home video market had become Italian cinema's prime outlet and much of its product was exploitation and cheap remakes like Ruggero Deodato's *The House on the Edge of the Park* (1980); a loose remake of *Last House on the Left* (1972) and Lucio Fulci's *Zombi 2* (1979); his unofficial sequel to *Dawn of the Dead* (1978). With *Conan the Barbarian* tearing up the box office in the US during the summer of 1982 and its Italian release pending in September, Italian filmmakers were hardly going to ignore the potential to capitalize on a new trend.

Their experience with pepla, low budget westerns, horror and caveman movies stood them in good stead and, rather than constructing sets, Italian movies tended to use real European castles and ruins for both interior and exterior shots contributing to a very different brand of sword and sorcery movie.

Gunan il guerriero (Gunan, King of the Barbarians) (1982)

Director: Francesco Prosperi (as Frank Shannon)
Writer: Piero Regnoli (story & screenplay) (as Peter Lombard)

Franco Prosperi had worked on the screenplays of two peplum movies in 1961; *La schiava di Roma* (*Slave of Rome*) and *Ercole al centro della terra* (*Hercules in the Haunted World*) but was best known for directing horror movies. As well as being one of the directors behind 1962's *Mondo cane* (often cited as the original 'Mondo film'), he directed a *Last House on the Left* knockoff called *Last House on the Beach* (1978) for producer Pino Buricchi.

Buricchi and Prosperi would also make the first of several Italian movies that capitalized on *Conan the Barbarian*'s success. *Gunan, King of the Barbarians* was rushed into production and beat the Italian release of *Conan the Barbarian* by a couple of days.

Starring the muscular Pietro Torrisi (billed here as Peter McCoy) – a stuntman with a long career of playing heavies and gladiators in many a peplum – the story begins as Conan's does; with a raid on a peaceful village. The object of the raid is a woman currently giving birth. According to a bewigged shaman, her son will be called 'Zukahn' as the stars have ordered it so, and he will be destined to fulfill the sacred prophecy and bring peace to the land. But lo! The woman is carrying twins!

The raid is led by the evil Nuriak (Emilio Messina) who, fearful that the prophecy is directed at him, beheads the woman and orders his men to search for what he presumes is her only son. But an elderly woman has slipped away with the two babes and, after making her way to the seashore, promptly dies of exhaustion.

A band of amazons turn up, looking for the prophesized child. They find the dead woman and the two babes but, not knowing which was born first, have no idea which of them is Zukahn.

After a rather abrupt jump forward, we are introduced to the two brothers twenty-odd years later. Raised by the amazons, one is called Gunan (Peter McCoy) while the other, played by Giovanni Cianfriglia, is apparently nameless, although ironically, he resembles Frazetta's version of Conan far more than McCoy does. The problem of the prophecy is a point of contention between the twins and can only be resolved by a series of trials. After Gunan wins, his envious brother slinks away and tries to take on Nuriak himself, getting himself beheaded in the process. Nuriak, thinking he has slain Zukahn and thus defied the prophecy, is unprepared for Gunan's quest for revenge.

That *Gunan* is incredibly low budget goes without saying and it pads out its very episodic plot by switching to slow motion every time somebody gets on a horse or swings a sword. The pacing isn't helped by altogether far too much narration and a lengthy prologue with dinosaur footage nabbed from Hammer's *One Million Years B.C.* (1966).

The movie also stars Sabrina Siani as the slave girl Lenni, whom Gunan rescues. Born Sabrina Seggiani in Rome, 1963, Siani is something of an Italian answer to

Lana Clarkson. Blonde, athletic and beautiful, Siani rarely starred in anything above cheap exploitation films. She was previously in *Mondo cannibale*; Franco Prosperi's 1980 collaboration with exploitation legend Jess Franco. As well as *Gunan* and the *Blue Lagoon* cash-in *Due gocce d'acqua salata* (*Blue Island*), 1982 also saw her star in *Ator the Fighting Eagle* and she would go on to appear in a total of five separate sword and sorcery movies in the 1980s, three of which paired her with fellow *Gunan* star Peter McCoy.

Ator l'invincible (Ator, the Fighting Eagle) (1982)

Director: Joe D'Amato (as David Hills)
Writer: Joe D'Amato (as David Hills)

Sabrina Siani's second sword and sorcery movie of 1982 was helmed by horror and sexploitation master Joe D'Amato, which is surprising given what a bloodless, boobless PG outing it is.

D'Amato probably worked under more pseudonyms than anybody else in the industry and directed around two-hundred movies. He occasionally blended horror and erotica as in *Erotic Nights of the Living Dead* (1980) and *Porno Holocaust* (1981). In 1980 he took over a production company from producer Ermanno Donati and renamed it 'Filmirage'. The first two movies slated were D'Amato's cult horror favorites *Antropophagus* (1980) and *Absurd* (1981). The third was the cut-rate (and PG) Conan imitator *Ator l'invincible (Ator the Fighting Eagle)*.

Miles O'Keeffe (whose single screen credit at this point was as the lead in the previous year's *Tarzan the Ape Man*) plays Ator, yet another child of prophecy who must be hidden from an evil tyrant. The tyrant in question is the High Priest of the Spider (played by Peruvian wrestler and actor, Dakar). His Herod-like efforts to wipe out all newborns fail when Ator, son of the mighty warrior Torren, is smuggled away by the banished priest Griba (Edmund Purdom). Griba gives him to a peasant family to raise as their own and makes sure to magically hide the 'Mark of Torren' on the baby's shoulder which will, of course, be used to identify him later on.

This all sounds more like *The Beastmaster* (1982) than *Conan the Barbarian* (1982); a comparison strengthened by the inclusion of a cute bear cub that accompanies our hero on his inevitable quest.

Ator grows to manhood and, rather strangely, falls in love with his sister, Sunya (Ritza Brown) *before* he finds out that he was adopted. Once the secret of his birth is revealed and the issue of incest is dismissed, the wedding plans go ahead but are cut short when the Spider Priest's warriors attack the village and carry off Sunya. Cue quest for revenge, and Ator sets off with the aforementioned bear cub.

While undergoing training with Griba (who is this movie's Obi-wan Kenobi to Ator's Luke Skywalker), Ator stops to rescue warrior woman Roon (Sabrina Siani) from some thugs. It turns out that Roon didn't need rescuing as she is a thief and she rides off with her stolen horses without so much as a thank you.

Apparently now ready to take on the Spider Priest, Ator sets out with his father's sword which Obi-wan, I mean, *Griba* has been safeguarding for him. Captured by amazons, Ator comes face to face with Roon again, who, as one of the amazons, is going to compete for the 'honor' of received Ator's seed and thus sireing the tribe's new leader.

Needless to say, Roon wins and, attracted both by Ator and the thought of robbing the Temple of the Spider God, she agrees to aid him on his quest. Their adventures involve evading a seductive sorceress and an encounter with the walking dead. Griba turns up again and instructs them to recover the magical shield of

Moordoor (no, not that one), with which they can defeat the Spider Priest.

Conan the Barbarian's influences are more evident here than they were in *Gunan, King of the Barbarians*. Not only is the villain the leader of an animal cult but Ator is seduced by a witch and teams up with a blonde warrior woman who joins him on his quest for revenge. Despite these similarities, *Ator* is more imaginative than *Gunan* although its minuscule budget and short running time stop it from being anything other than a shallow *Conan* cash-in.

Sangraal, la spada di fuoco (Sword of the Barbarians) (1982)

Director: Michele Massimo Tarantini (as Michael E. Lemick)

Writer: Michele Massimo Tarantini (story), Piero Regnoli (screenplay), Ted Rusoff (dialogue supervisor)

Gunan, King of the Barbarians producer Pino Buricchi was able to squeeze a second sword and sorcery adventure in between the Italian release of *Conan the Barbarian* and 1982's end. Reuniting *Gunan* stars Peter McCoy and Sabrina Siani, the directing reigns were handed over to Michele Massimo Tarantini whose resume consisted of a string of giallo films and sex comedies.

McCoy plays Sangraal who, if the prologue is to be believed, is the son of King Ator. *That* Ator? We never find out. By reusing footage from the opening attack of *Gunan*, Sangraal is given a near identical origin story. Smuggled out of the massacre by his nursemaid, Sangraal grows up to become the leader of a nomadic people looking for a new home.

Their way leads them through an eerie desert marked by skeletons wired to posts which they surmise "can only be the work of an evil and bloodthirsty race". Unnerved, the tribe wants to turn back but Sangraal urges them on. "Land belongs to anyone who can cultivate it!" he blusters, revealing a rather colonial attitude for a barbarian hero. Then, displaying a degree of cultural insensitivity, they tear down everything in sight before moving on.

They come across a village under attack by Nantuk (Mario Novelli as Anthony Freeman) – the very warlord who slaughtered Sangraal's village – and Sangraal wades in, sword swinging. The grateful villagers offer them shelter and the chieftain's daughter Aki (Yvonne Fraschetti) seems particularly moony-eyed over Sangraal, despite his wife being on hand.

Meanwhile, Nantuk is passing the time by casting young naked women to the flames in sacrifice to Rani, the goddess of fire and death (Xiomara Rodriguez). Rani informs Nantuk of Sangraal's existence and orders him to be destroyed.

A second raid on the village is more successful and Sangraal is hoisted up on a cross and forced to witness the village's destruction and the massacre of its inhabitants, including his wife. Aki rescues Sangraal with the aid of wandering archer Li Wo Twan (Hal Yamanouchi, credited here as Al Huang, who has since appeared in 2013's *The Wolverine*). Sangraal wants to bring his wife back to life. Twan suggests that Rudak the sage might be able to help and so, Sangraal and his companions make their way to the Black Mountains to seek him out. The influence of *Conan the Barbarian* is clear in the trio of muscular barbarian, Asian archer and attractive warrior woman.

After some misadventures, they find Rudak (Massimo Pittarello) who explains that he is unable to bring back the dead but, if Sangraal wants revenge against Nantuk and his goddess, he must seek out the 'Ark of the Templars' which contains the weapon required for the job.

The ark, kept hidden in a cave, is guarded by the Goddess of Gold and Life (Sabrina Siani in little more than a cameo role). She isn't about to let Sangraal just take the weapon so Rudak turns up in a cloud of green smoke and clears the way for our hero. Now able to open the ark, Sangraal pulls out an enormous crossbow. Which is handy as Nantuk's men have just arrived and carried off Aki.

As with *Gunan*, *Sangraal* is still hampered by its cheapness and is shot almost entirely outdoors with almost no sets apart from the occasional small village or cave lair. This simplicity sets Pino Buricchi's sword and sorcery movies apart from the marginally more accomplished Ator movies.

Hercules (1983)

Director: Luigi Cozzi (as Lewis Coates)
Writer: Luigi Cozzi (as Lewis Coates)

If there is one cinematic predecessor to Conan, then it is surely Hercules. One of our oldest sword and sorcery heroes, Hercules (or 'Heracles' to give him his Greek name) was the result of Zeus having his sneaky way with Queen Alcmene of Thebes by pretending to be her husband. Enraged by yet another infidelity, Zeus's wife Hera sent a pair of snakes to kill the child, but the infant demi-god succeeded in strangling one in each hand.

Heracles (who's birth name was Alcides) had a troubled youth and, in a fit of madness (possibly caused by the still-vengeful Hera), murdered his wife and children. Seeking guidance from the Oracle of Delphi, Alcides changed his name to Heracles (meaning 'glory of Hera') in an effort to placate the goddess and embarked on a series of ten trials for his enemy, King Eurystheus, by way of penance. These trials largely involved defeating monsters like the Nemean Lion and the nine-headed Hydra. King Eurystheus disqualified Heracles from two of the tasks and set him new ones, resulting in the twelve labors Heracles best known for.

Many other feats and adventures were attributed to Heracles and the Romans enjoyed the character so much they came up with their own tales, renaming him 'Hercules'. Italy was home to the character once again in the peplum boom following Steve Reeves's popular 1957 portrayal, but the genre fizzled in the mid-sixties. After Arnold Schwarzenegger became a cinematic titan with the success of *Conan the Barbarian* (1982), notorious knock-off merchants, Cannon Films, began eyeing up the potential of his *Pumping Iron* costar, Lou Ferrigno for a similar meteoric career.

Ferrigno, who was picked on at school for his significant loss of hearing due to childhood ear infections, was a big fan of Steve Reeves and his Hercules movies. Following in Reeves's footsteps, Ferrigno became a bodybuilder and then an actor. By 1982, his run on TV as *The Incredible Hulk* was over and he eagerly accepted a couple of roles in Cannon's quick Conan cash-ins.

Produced by Cannon's Italian production arm (Cannon Italia Srl), *Hercules* was shot back to back with *The Seven Magnificent Gladiators,* sharing several of its stars (although curiously, none of its sets). *Hercules* is a dizzying disco-inspired extravaganza that has the gods living on the moon and a female Daedalus who builds giant robots that shoot lasers. The origin of its titular character is played about with too; this time he is sent by Zeus to aid humankind in their time of trial against evil. Hercules is a hero "practically invincible, made from the purest of all energies; light!" incarnated in the body of the son of the King of Thebes.

But there is skullduggery afoot in Thebes. Adriana (Sybil Danning) overthrows the king and queen with the help of the palace guard and steals the sacred sword of Thebes. Baby Hercules is smuggled out by a servant girl who is shot down just as she places him into a boat.

Hercules is washed, Moses-like, down river to be retrieved by a kind, childless couple who raise him as their own. This is just after he strangles the two snakes Hera (Rossana Podestà) sends to slay him. Quite why Hera despises Hercules in this version which does away with Zeus's rape of Queen Alcmene is a mystery, but it has something to do with 'righting the balance'. The gods continually mess with poor Hercules throughout the movie.

Hercules grows up into a man of superhuman strength. We see him rip a tree out of the ground and then battle a bear that has slain his father (a scene comprised of a man in a terrible bear costume and recycled footage from the 1976 *Jaws* knock-off *Grizzly*). Hercules is so strong that he hurls the bear into orbit in perhaps the most laughable scene of the movie.

The bear was apparently sent by Hera who still hasn't given up. She then orders her devoted follower, the science-obsessed King Minos (William Berger) to slay Hercules. Minos outsources this to Daedalus (Eva Robins) who sends one of her mechanical monsters. The monster kills Hercules's mother, leaving the orphaned hero wondering why everybody hates him so much.

He winds up at the court of King Augeias (Brad Harris who played Hercules in 1962's *The Fury of Hercules*) where he wins a fighting tournament and then hurls a log into orbit (which seems to be his signature move). Impressed, King Augeias hires him to escort his beautiful daughter Cassiopeia (Ingrid Anderson) to Athens. But first, to further prove his worth, Hercules has to muck out the stables.

This is one of the mythical twelve labors and, true to legend, Hercules diverts a river, allowing it to wash through the stables and clear out the accumulated dung of a thousand horses. Cassiopeia, a tad smitten by

Hercules, removes her veil and kisses him. Apparently, choosing his own lover isn't what Zeus had in mind for the savior of mankind so he stuns them both with a lightening bolt. Adriana (who, we learn, is the daughter of King Minos) turns up and kidnaps them both.

Cassiopeia is to be taken to the isle of Thera and its capital of Atlantis where she will be sacrificed to Hera. Hercules is loaded with chains and tossed overboard. He survives and washes up on an island ruled by the haggard sorceress Circe (Mirella D'Angelo). Convincing Hercules to give her a few drops of his blood, Circe transforms into her beautiful younger self and together the pair set off on a series of adventures including defeating Daedalus's mechanical hydra (which has three heads instead of nine, presumably due to the budget), as well as taking a trip across the River Styx to the Underworld.

Determined to rescue Cassiopeia, Hercules journeys to Thera where King Minos has captured the mythical phoenix and imprisoned it in the mountain (which is now an active volcano). The fire is the source of Minos's power, but it requires regular sacrificial offerings, hence the capture of Cassiopeia. Hercules is imprisoned and Minos sends his daughter, Adriana, to seduce him in order to produce a race of supreme champions. But Ferrigno's joyless, puritan Hercules is having none of that and he breaks his chains to rescue Cassiopeia.

Despite Cannon's aim to ape the success of the R-rated *Conan the Barbarian*, *Hercules* was a PG affair, largely a result of Lou Ferrigno's rejection of the original script which was much more adult in tone (15). Nevertheless, Luigi Cozzi, who had directed the bizarre Italian *Star Wars* knock off *Starcrash* (1978) brings a certain neon vibrancy to a thoroughly pedestrian version of the Hercules legend and, heavily promoted upon release, the movie was a modest hit for Cannon.

I sette magnifici gladiatori (The Seven Magnificent Gladiators) (1983)

Director: Bruno Mattei

Writer: Claudio Fragasso (screenplay) (as Claude Fragass)

Filmed at the same time as *Hercules* (1983) this remake of *Seven Samurai/The Magnificent Seven* sets the story in antiquity where a band of villains led by Nicerote (Dan Vadis who had played Hercules in a couple of pepla in the 1960s) terrorizes the peaceful community of Clusium (filmed amid the ruins of Ostia Antica).

The movie also features Lou Ferrigno's wife and manager, Carla Ferrigno in her first screen role as Pandora, a gutsy woman from Clusium who sets out on a quest to find help. The village's matriarch (who is revealed to be Nicerote's mother) gives her a magic sword and instructions to seek out the one man who can wield it. That man is currently in Rome so Pandora and several of her friends head for the city with the sword wrapped in a blanket.

Perhaps the most off-model Roman emperor in cinema history (played by Cannon regular Yehuda Efroni) is enjoying a chariot race between two old friends (and *Hercules* costars); Han (Lou Ferrigno) and Scipio (Brad Harris). Defying the emperor's orders to fight to the death, Han and Scipio flee, prompting the enraged emperor to send out his guards to apprehend them.

Meanwhile, Pandora and co. have arrived in Rome and put the first man they see to the test; a cheeky and boastful chap (comic relief alert!) called Vendrix. As soon as he grasps the sword, Vendrix's hands start smoking and the sword's hilt glows red. It turns out that only the chosen one can wield it.

Fortunately, the chosen one (Han) and his companion Scipio are on hand to rescue Pandora and her companions from being assaulted by a band of lepers. But before Han can be put to the test, soldiers capture the lot of them and bring them before the emperor.

Upon learning of the magic sword, the foolish emperor assumes that he must be its chosen one. As soon as he holds it, the same thing happens as before, leaving him clutching his scorched hand. Pandora tosses the sword to Han who has no problem holding it and proceeds to knock over all the emperor's guards in one of the movie's thoroughly bloodless scraps. The companions flee Rome along with Scipio's warrior lady friend Julia (Sybil Danning).

Stopping off at a tavern to celebrate their escape, they recruit two ex-gladiators called Festo and Glafiro. Lo and behold, the emperor's soldiers turn up prompting a tavern fight and another hasty escape. Vendrix, apparently friends with Han and the other gladiators, turns up to help out, making them a party of six. The seventh magnificent gladiator is picked up on the way to Clusium; a beefy giant called Goliath (Emilio Messina who played the wicked Nuriak in *Gunan, King of the Barbarians*).

With its outdoor locations, short running time and near total lack of special effects, *The Seven Magnificent Gladiators* was very much a B movie to its A movie counterpart *Hercules*. As with most variations on the *Seven Samurai* plot, seven is rather a lot of characters for an 80-minute movie and there isn't much of a chance to get to know any of them much less remember their names. Director Bruno Mattei, who had previously helmed a bunch of Nazisploitation and women in prison pictures, struggles to come up with anything new in this ultra-low budget variation on a well-worn story.

Thor il conquistatore (Thor the Conqueror) (1983)

Director: Tonino Ricci (as Anthony Richmond)
Writer: Tito Carpi

One of the decade's more obscure efforts was *Thor il conquistatore* (*Thor the Conqueror*), although any relation to the Norse god of thunder (or his Marvel incarnation) is left unestablished.

Thor is born to the usual tune of mumbled prophecies but, as his proud father lifts him into the air, an arrow thuds into the newborn's writhing form, setting the tone for the rest of this particularly cheap and nasty entry in a genre known for cheap nastiness.

Luckily, the wizard Etna (Luigi Mezzanotte as Christopher Holm) is on hand to whisk the infant away as his parents are butchered by attacking barbarians. Thor (Bruno Minniti as Conrad Nichols) survives his arrow wound and grows to manhood apparently in such isolation that he has no idea what a woman is until he is called upon to rescue one from a band of thugs. This act of heroism is somewhat spoilt when Thor drags her back to his cave and rapes her in a scene that makes Deathstalker look like Galahad. Etna watches the whole thing while making comments like "what else is she good for?" and "the female has to obey her master. It is proven." With a parent like that, it's no wonder Thor's moral compass is a little skewed.

Now, having "known a woman and killed a man", Thor is ready to go forth and unearth the blade of his father in the name of the god Teisha and exact his revenge. The almost total absence of sets in this movie mean that Thor spends over an hour of the running time aimlessly wandering through forests and hills having various encounters. He fights some warrior women (who wear wicker baskets on their heads) and, after defeating their leader, rapes and enslaves her.

Her name is Ina (Maria Romana whose career fared little better with movies like *Violence in a Women's Prison* and *Women's Prison Massacre*). She is able to escape her bonds while Thor is busy being captured by some painted cultists. Then, rather implausibly, she rescues him, apparently bowled over by his charms and kind nature.

Now star-crossed lovers, Thor and Ina journey on and are taken in by a kindly tribe who, recognizing Thor's strength and courage, make him their leader as well as the stud for all their young women. Such a blissful existence is cut short by the arrival of the villainous Gnut (Raf Baldassarre as Raf Falcone), the very man who slew Thor's parents.

Recognizing him as the baby he tried to slay many years ago (by a birthmark on his neck he couldn't possibly have seen at that distance), Gnut blinds Thor and casts him adrift to wander aimlessly. This doesn't present much of a problem because old Etna is on hand to restore his sight via a mixture of snake venom and moss. Conjuring a horse for Thor out of thin air, Etna sends him off to find his father's sword (which was buried with him) and exact his vengeance on the dastardly Gnut.

Il trono di fuoco (Throne of Fire) (1983)

Director: Francesco Prosperi (as Franco Prosperi)

Writer: Giuseppe Buricchi (story), Nino Marino (story and screenplay)

Gunan, King of the Barbarians director Franco Prosperi reunited with Sabrina Siani and Peter McCoy for a second sword and sorcery romp (McCoy and Siani's third together) called *Il trono di fuoco* (*Throne of Fire*). Don't be fooled by any claims that this is even loosely based on the medieval German epic *The Nibelungenlied*. Aside from the hero being called 'Siegfried' and the heroine 'Valkari', there is nothing about dwarven treasure, magic rings or even dragons in this rather gloomy entry mostly filmed at Castello Orsini-Odescalchi in Bracciano, Italy, which has played host to many movies over the years including *The Agony and the Ecstasy* (1965) and the original *The Inglorious Bastards* (1978).

Serving girl Azira (Benny Cardoso) is visited by the devil himself (Harrison Muller) who rapes her, claiming that his son must sit upon the titular Throne of Fire and rule the world. We next see her crashing through the woods, seeking shelter from a storm. She finds it in a muddy cave where she gives birth to a nasty, rubbery creature.

Meanwhile, back at the castle, another baby is born by the name of Siegfried. His parents already have him pegged as a hero for there is a prophecy that he will foil an evil usurper one day. An additional element of the prophecy is that no one may sit on the Throne of Fire without being incinerated unless they do so during the 'day of the night of the day' (a solar eclipse).

Flash forward a couple of decades and that ghastly rubber puppet Azira gave birth to has grown up to be a handsome lad called Morak (also played by Harrison Muller). His mother, who, despite her initial reluctance to the devil's plan, seems to wholeheartedly support it now, instructs him in what he must do and he sets off to usurp the king and worm his way into the line of succession by marrying the king's daughter, Princess Valkari (Sabrina Siani).

We then get a couple of scenes of carnage nabbed from *Gunan, King of the Barbarians* and *Sword of the Barbarians* which are presumably meant to depict Morak's rise to power. New footage reveals that his forces locate and capture Princess Valkari, who has been hiding with some peasants, and haul her away for a date with the devil.

Siegfried (Peter McCoy) arrives on the scene a tad too late but heads for the castle where Morak now reigns. He sneaks into the forced wedding dressed as a priest, intending to throw a spanner in the works. Confronting Morak, Siegfried stabs him to no effect. As well as learning that the tyrant is seemingly invulnerable, Siegfried also gets a glimpse of the real demon behind the man.

Refusing Morak's offer of employment, Siegfried is thrown into the 'well of madness'. Spooky visions ensue and Siegfried battles a spectral black knight before finding his father whom he thought had been slain. Made invisible by his father (who is apparently a sorcerer), Siegfried teams up with Princess Valkari and goes forth to battle Morak and restore peace to the land.

More King Arthur than Conan, *Throne of Fire* plays with several plot devices of medieval romance such as invisibility spells, haunted suits of armor and talk of the actual devil rather than made up pagan cults.

Conquest (1983)

Director: Lucio Fulci

Writer: Giovanni Di Clemente (story), Gino Capone (screenplay) José Antonio de la Loma (screenplay) Carlos Vasallo screenplay)

Lucio Fulci was the director of many controversial horror and giallo movies that have since become cult classics like *Non si sevizia un paperino (Don't Torture a Duckling)* (1972), *Zombi 2* (1979) and *...E tu vivrai nel terrore! L'aldilà, lit (The Beyond)* (1981). His 1983 sword and sorcery movie has also become something of a cult classic, not because it is on par with those entries, but for its sheer, unfathomable weirdness.

Shot in a very soft focus, the film has a surreal, dreamlike quality where everything is misty and ethereal. The rambling plot's casual approach to logic only adds to the effect of alternating dream and nightmare.

It opens in a rather Greek-looking land of mist and translucency, presumably intended to convey paradise. The young warrior Ilias is given a magic bow (that occasionally glows a neon blue) by his father and dispatched on some sort of rite of passage quest. He sets off in his boat and arrives in a decidedly darker place ruled by the evil queen Ocron (Sabrina Siani who, in a strange choice on the part of the filmmakers, wears a mask for the whole movie, if very little else). Her werewolf-type followers terrorize the primitive natives and bring back the head of a girl for Ocron who then cracks it open and devours the brain within (the gore in this movie is certainly true to Fulci form).

Meanwhile, Ilias has gotten himself into a scrape already after saving a girl from a snake and then being attacked by Ocron's minions. He is aided by a rather more heroic-looking figure, Mace (Jorge Rivero) who wields nunchaku fashioned from bones.

Mace takes Ilias to some cave people he knows and Ilias is pleased to see the girl he saved earlier. But any budding romance between the two is spoiled by another attack from Ocron's wolfmen who kill the girl and capture Ilias. Mace tracks the party and rescues him by tossing a rock (that inexplicably explodes) at his captors and then massacring the rest.

Deciding that Ocron must pay for her crimes, Mace and Ilias venture on but are assailed by a cackling bush that shoots spines at them. Ilias is struck and the wound festers, causing him to break out in nasty pustules. Mace goes off to look for the plant that can heal him (fighting zombies on the way) while Ilias is nearly killed by Mace's doppelganger (really a demon conjured by Ocron). The real Mace turns up in the nick of time and slays his double.

Rather fed up with everything, Ilias decides to return to his homeland. On his lonesome, Mace is captured by some very strange-looking creatures who would be more at home in an old Doctor Who episode. In keeping with what had become a trope of the genre by this point, they tie him to a cross. Probably trying to echo *Conan the Barbarian* (or perhaps *Spartacus*) rather than Jesus Christ, the crucifixion scene appears in many sword and sorcery movies, from Talon's crucifixion over dinner in the *The Sword and the Sorcerer* to Peter

McCoy being hoisted up in both *Sword of the Barbarians* and *Throne of Fire*.

Ilias, who has had a change of heart, returns to shoot a few laser arrows into the creatures in an effort to save his friend but is unable to stop Mace (still tied to the cross) from tumbling into the sea. In one of the movie's more inexplicable moments, dolphins appear and nibble through his bonds, freeing him.

Reunited, Ilias and Mace continue their quest to topple Ocron, but there is still plenty of weirdness and nonsensical plot points to come before the final showdown with the topless queen.

Ator 2: L'invincibile Orion (The Blade Master) (1984)

Director: Joe D'Amato (as David Hills)
Writer: Uncredited

With the commercial success of the first Ator movie, a sequel was hastily thrown into production with Miles O'Keeffe back in the title role but there isn't much to connect it to the previous installment. It opens with some grunting cavepeople banging bones together and eating lice out of each other's hair before they are attacked by another clan.

The scene is a slightly more civilized one at the 'Castle of the Great One' (Castello Piccolomini, Balsorano, L'Aquila, Italy). The alchemist Akronos (Charles Borromel) has discovered an element that can be a tool of great good or great evil ("It all depends on man. What man does with it"). Which is bad news as the evil mustachioed Zor and his forces are sweeping south. There is only one man who can protect it. Ator! (cue reused footage with voiceover recapping the events of the first movie). We then catch up with Ator during one of his workout sessions. He has retired to the eastern lands where he trains with his wise friend Thong (Kiro Wehara as Chen Wong).

As Zor's Hun-like minions capture the castle, Akronos sends his daughter Mila (Lisa Foster) to fetch Ator. Zor (David Brandon as David Cain Haughton) wants the weapon Akronos has discovered but Akronos has hidden it. This might spell bad news for Akronos but, as he was once Zor's tutor, Zor is reluctant to torture him.

Mila fights her way through Zor's guards but receives an arrow in the hand. She makes it to Ator and Thong's lair where they nurse her back to health. Ator is portrayed as a thinking man's barbarian, more at home in his lab surrounded by bubbling test tubes and crucibles than on the battlefield. Once a pupil of Akronos, Ator is knowledgeable in medicine and smithery (possibly the source of the movie's U.S. title *The Blade Master*).

Setting off to thwart Zor and rescue Akronos, Ator, Thong and Mila (another echo of *Conan the Barbarian*'s triumvirate of Conan, Subotai and Valeria) get separated in some fog summoned by Zor's dark sorcerer. Ator and Thong battle invisible warriors while Mila is captured by a tribe of cannibalistic cavemen. Ator rescues her, dazzling them with an explosion.

The companions are then attacked by some warriors in samurai garb, furthering the eastern flavor of this particular entry. These warriors, we later learn in an unexpected but welcome bit of backstory, are survivors of the noble tribe of Han who worshipped the god of war. The tribe's leader was usurped by his own brother, Zor.

Their path leads them close to Ator's home village where they learn that an evil nomadic people called the Kungs have arrived in Ator's absence and have been demanding sacrificial offerings for their snake god. Ator is about to rally the villagers *Seven Samurai* style but betrayal is afoot, and his drink is drugged by the village elder. He wakes up to find himself tied to a post alongside Mila (Thong having somehow snuck off).

The Kungs arrive to claim their tribute. They are of course, in league with Zor and bring Ator and Mila to him. In the bowels of some unidentified lair, the sacrifice begins with some girls being tossed into a snake pit as some sort of appetizer. Thong appears and sneakily cuts Ator's bonds so that he is able to intervene before Mila joins the other girls in the pit. She gets tossed in during the scuffle anyway, prompting Ator to leap in and save her by fighting a giant rubber snake.

The trio make for the Castle of the Great One to take Zor to task for his crimes. While Thong and Mila sneak in via an underground passage, Ator shows off his scientific mind once more by hastily knocking together a thoroughly modern-looking hang glider which he uses to drop homemade grenades on the castle's defenders before landing and hacking his way to a final fight with Zor.

Science and philosophy play a large role in this outing with a rather obvious parallel drawn between Akronos's discovery and the atom bomb. Sorcery is almost non-existent with crude science and alchemy filling in for magic which makes for an interesting take on the genre.

Le avventure dell'incredibile Ercole
(The Adventures of Hercules) (1985)

Director: Luigi Cozzi (as Lewis Coates)
Writer: Luigi Cozzi (as Lewis Coates)

Hercules (1983) may not have been met with much warmth critically speaking but it pulled in enough money for Cannon to send Lou Ferrigno out on another adventure as Hercules.

After a lengthy title sequence intercut with clips of Hercules showing off his might from the previous movie, we are given the setup. Four of the gods, resentful of being under Zeus's command, have stolen his seven thunderbolts. This has caused chaos to reign and the moon (which, if you'll recall, is where Mount Olympus is situated) is currently hurtling towards Earth. Only by retrieving the thunderbolts can order be restored, but they are hidden within the bellies of various monsters who dwell in dangerous places, providing a rather lazy setup for Hercules's new quest.

This time, Herc is joined by two scantily clad companions; Urania (Milly Carlucci) and Glaucia (Sonia Viviani) who belong to a tribe currently threatened by a fire beast to which their flamboyant priest is regularly sacrificing virgins. Seeking out Hercules, Urania and Glaucia accompany him on his quest to find the seven thunderbolts of Zeus.

But Hera and the other gods are up to no good once more and, in a scene reminiscent of a Hammer Dracula movie, they resurrect the villain from the previous movie – King Minos (William Berger) – by dripping blood onto his dusty bones.

Hercules, having already collected the first lightening bolt on his own by defeating a man in an ape suit, meets up with Urania and Glaucia and battles 'the Slime People' (more monster suits) before passing into 'the Forbidden Valley' where a stop-motion gorgon lurks. The scene is copied wholesale from *Clash of the Titans* (1981) although Ray Harryhausen is so far from this movie that he might as well be a moon-dwelling Olympian.

Meanwhile, Minos is planning on double-crossing the gods and calls upon his old pal Daedalus (Eva Robins again) who gives him a magical ice sword with which he can defeat them.

After slaying the demon Tartarus (who wields a green laser trident), Hercules finds that he must chase after another MacGuffin; a balm from the sanctuary of Thetis which will shield him from the flames of the fire beast. Leaving Glaucia on the beach, Hercules and Urania journey under the sea and return to find that Glaucia has been abducted by the high-priest of their tribe. After Hercules makes short work of the fire beast and rescues Glaucia, the race is on to find the rest of the thunderbolts while Minos wages his war against the gods.

Hercules never seems to have to travel very far or do anything much to find these monsters, they just sort of turn up and he summarily defeats them. The slashed budget is evident although Cozzi takes the neon and laser look of the first movie and dials it up to eleven. There is even some cheeky rotoscoping of scenes from other movies such as the electrical fire monster (clearly nabbed from 1956's *Forbidden Planet*) and the bizarre climax where Hercules and King Minos inexplicably morph into a giant ape and a T. Rex in a fight that suspiciously resembles the famous scene from *King Kong* (1933).

Ator il guerriero di ferro (Iron Warrior) (1987)

Director: Alfonso Brescia (as Al Bradley)

Writer: Steven Luotto (story & screenplay), Alfonso Brescia (story & screenplay) (as Al Bradley)

Miles O'Keeffe would return to the role of Ator one more time in what is essentially a prequel to the whole saga, that is, *if* you chose to see the movies as connected series (and that really is optional due to their continuity being rather thin). Another reason to discount this one as 'cannon' is that it is the only Ator movie not made by Joe D'Amato. *Iron Warrior* was instead directed by Alfonso Brescia (as Al Bradley), the man behind a handful of peplum and giallo flicks plus five *Star Wars* knockoffs including *War of the Planets* (1977) and *Battle of the Stars* (1978).

It opens with two boys playing ball in some old ruins. A sinister woman appears and snatches one of them away before vanishing. This displeases a group of mysterious women referred to as her 'sisters' (either goddesses or a cult of very powerful sorceresses). The kidnapper, whom we learn is called Phoadre (Elizabeth Kaza), faces some sort of trial for her crime. One of the sisters – Deeva (Iris Peynado) – claims to have created the two boys for a purpose; to protect a princess whose birth is imminent. The sisters demand that the stolen boy is returned. Phoadre refuses and is banished to the 'Underlands' for eighteen years and is imprisoned in a spinning neon hula hoop very reminiscent of *Superman* (1978).

Eighteen years is just enough time for the remaining boy to grow to manhood and become the mighty warrior Ator (with a much less shaggy haircut now). If his sword looks a little familiar, that's because it is a replica of the Atlantean sword from *Conan the Barbarian* and, as rumor has it, was repainted and wielded by Ralf Moeller in the 1997 TV series *Conan the Adventurer*. Also reaching adulthood at the same time is the princess Janna (Savina Gersak), whose eighteenth birthday celebrations are interrupted by the arrival of Phoadre and her servant, the titular Iron Warrior; a towering giant in a silver skull mask who begins chopping people up. The king sends Janna to fetch help just before his own impalement at the hands of the Iron Warrior.

Phoadre isn't about to let Ator stick his oar in her plans and disguises herself as a damsel in a turquoise dress in need of rescue. Ator saves her from being attacked and then spends the night with her. Phoadre sneaks out while he is asleep and tries to burn down the house down with him inside. He is saved by a vision from Deeva who tells him that he must travel to the land of Dragor where the one he is destined to protect awaits.

En route, Ator comes across the unconscious form of the Princess Jenna who has been captured by some zombie monks and placed on an altar. He chases the monks off and is then confronted by the Iron Warrior himself. Defeating him, the Iron Warrior collapses into a pile of clothes, apparently just a vision sent by Phoadre.

Ator takes the now conscious Jenna to what looks like a cemetery and leaves her there while he goes on to find out what's up at her father's court. Upon arrival he is greeted by the king and his courtiers who attempt to dissuade him that anything is amiss. But Ator spies the woman in turquoise he rescued earlier and knows that everything is another of Phoadre's shams. He finds himself battling the Iron Warrior once more. Jenna pops up and helps him escape (although it's probably wise to suspect everybody at this point).

Some cat-and-mouse fights with Phoadre's soldiers are followed by a surreal sequence involving Jenna's dress changing from red to turquoise (dress colors are significant in this movie). At a dire moment, Deeva spirits Ator and Jenna away to an underground cavern where she explains a few things. Firstly, the Iron Warrior is none other than Ator's kidnapped brother Trogar, now a shell of a man under Phoadre's power. Secondly, the only way to destroy Phoadre is to recover the Golden Chest of the Ages from the sunken Isle of Stygian.

The style of this third entry is radically different from previous Italian sword and sorcery movies. Better cinematography, vibrant colors and hair and makeup that border on cyberpunk make this a fresher, younger and prettier little brother to the previous Ator movies. The many ruins on the Maltese island of Gozo are put to good use (even if the iron handrails put up for tourists are visible in some shots) and overall, the movie is reminiscent of the more glossy sword and sorcery fare that was produced for television in the nineties.

Sinbad of the Seven Seas (1989)

Director: Enzo G. Castellari

Writer: Tito Carpi, Enzo G. Castellari (screenplay), Luigi Cozzi (as Lewis Coates) (story)

Originally shot in 1986 as part of Lou Ferrigno's run of sword and sorcery movies for Cannon Films, the project was shelved when Cannon started heading for bankruptcy and the money for the special effects ran out. This is according to director Enzo Castellari who later spotted his own movie on video cassette and learned that it had been completed on the cheap without his knowledge.[23]

Cannon, never ones to waste an opportunity, had hired Luigi Cozzi to complete the movie by shooting extra scenes that bypassed the need for special effects. One of these is the movie's opening where a mother in the present day (Daria Nicolodi) is reading a bedtime story to her little girl (Cozzis' own daughter). The title of the book she is reading is 'Edgar Allen Poe's Sinbad'. According to the movie's prologue, this movie is based on his story *The Thousand-and-Second Tale of Scheherazade*, a darkly humorous sequel to the *One Thousand and One Nights* in which Scheherazade pushes her luck by relating one final tale of Sinbad to her murderous husband who then has her put to death the following morning for telling such outrageous lies. But nothing in Scheherazade's tale of Sinbad bears any resemblance to *Sinbad of the Seven Seas*, except maybe the appearance of a hot air balloon.

With that nonsense out of the way, we are dropped into the adventure. Sinbad and his motley crew are accompanying Prince Ali (Roland Wybenga) to the port city of Basra where he is to marry Princess Alina (Alessandra Martines). The unbelievably hammy evil vizier Jaffar (John Steiner) has hypnotized the elderly caliph and wants to force the princess to marry him instead of Prince Ali. The similarity to Disney's *Aladdin* (1992) is striking but both movies pilfer liberally from 1940's *The Thief of Bagdad*.

Sinbad (Ferrigno in purple spandex leggings) goes to the palace and is thrown into a snake pit while Jaffar sends out his soldiers to arrest his crew which consists of a Viking (Ennio Girolami), a cook (Yehuda Efroni), a kung-fu expert (*Sword of the Barbarians*'s Hal Yamanouchi) and a dwarf called 'Poochie' (Cork Hubbert). They are hauled off to the dungeons for torture, but Sinbad comes to the rescue after charming the snakes in his cell and tying them together to make a rather rubbery escape rope.

After knocking all the guards into a tank of piranhas (except one who voluntarily jumps in after being set on fire, and another who gets hurled into an iron maiden), Sinbad and his crew meet up with Poochie the dwarf (or is that 'Pucci'? – this is an Italian movie, after all), who has snuck into Jaffar's chambers and learned of his evil intentions. As well as imprisoning Princess Alina in a rather modern looking machine made of Perspex designed to drain her life force, he has also stolen the four magical stones of Basra and hidden them in dangerous places guarded by powerful forces; a plot setup that will sound familiar to anyone who has seen Lou Ferrigno's previous fantasy romp; *The Adventures of Hercules* (1985).

The scenes that follow hint at the movie's troubled production. Mom's voiceover picks up the slack to cover for scenes that were never filmed and before we know it, Sinbad and co. are battling the undead out on the open ocean. A visit to an oracle reveals the location of the four magic stones and Sinbad embarks on an episodic series of adventures to recover them, helped along by Mom's narration and clips from Ferrigno's *Hercules* movies. He battles a rock monster, gets hypnotized by the queen of a tribe of amazons, fights some empty suits of armor on the Isle of the Dead and is then separated from his crew by Jaffar's meddling sorcery. After defeating a slime monster that shoots laser bolts from its hands, Sinbad retrieves the last stone and returns to Basra (by inflating a hot air balloon with his lungs), for a final showdown against a clone of himself created by Jaffar.

Despite its shortcomings, *Sinbad of the Seven Seas* at least *looks* better than Lou Ferrigno's previous Cannon adventures. The locations are more impressive and populated with more extras and one can't help but feel that if the movie had been completed properly, it would have outpaced the other entries in Ferrigno's sword and sorcery quartet by several Herculean miles.

Il signore di Akili (Quest for the Mighty Sword) (1990)

Director: Joe D'Amato (as David Hills)
Writer: Joe D'Amato (as David Hills)

Apparently none too impressed with Alfonso Brescia's Ator prequel, Joe D'Amato knocked out one final Ator movie with his original company Filmirage, although this time *sans* Miles O'Keeffe.

There are two Ators in this movie; Prince Ator (who dies before the ten-minute mark) and his son, also called Ator, who embarks upon the titular quest. Both are played by Eric Allen Kramer (Little John in *Robin Hood: Men in Tights*) and, as Miles O'Keeffe is nowhere in sight, we are left wondering if this is a sequel to the previous movies or an alternate prequel that overrides *Iron Warrior*.

Prince Ator (why not 'King Ator'?) rules the land of Aquiles and is the kind of ruler who likes to dispense justice personally by engaging criminals in single combat. We see him dispatch a couple of ne'er-do-wells with his mighty 'Sword of Grahhl'. This sword is greatly desired by Thorn, the king of the gods, who turns up at court and kills Ator, shattering his mighty sword in the same blow. Warrior woman Dejanira (Margaret Lenzey) tries to intervene, which upsets the sisters of her order and, as punishment for defying the will of the gods, she is imprisoned behind a wall of fire to await the day a man strong and brave enough can rescue her.

Years later, Ator the Younger is fully grown and lives with the troll Grindl. He learns from the witch Nephele (Marisa Mell), that his mother took the fragments of his father's broken sword to Grindl and instructed him to re-forge it and give it to Ator on his eighteenth birthday. The lecherous little Grindl demanded a rather carnal payment for this and Ator's mother replied to the effect that she would rather die.

Grindl offered to help her with this and brewed up a poison. But Grindl double-crossed her, slipping her some sort of drug that made her offer herself to him, meaning that he got to have his way with her after all. This vile experience drove Ator's mother mad and now she wanders the land aimlessly "condemned to repeat her sin eternally".

Ator, who believed his mother was dead, is understandably peeved by this revelation. He picks up the Sword of Grahhl and takes a swing at Grindl's head. The sword shatters and Grindle cackles. The sword was a fake. Ator sees a vision of Dejanira and learns that only with the Sword of Grahhl can he cross the fire and rescue her, so he determines to find the shards of the real sword and re-forge it himself.

He does this and then slices Grindl in half, which isn't as bloody as it sounds. As the titular quest for the sword is now complete with two thirds of the movie's running time left, a second MacGuffin is required. Nephele tells Ator that not even the sword is enough to defeat Thorn. Only by offering the 'Treasure of the Kingdom of the West' to the gods can Ator have his vengeance.

This treasure is guarded by mechanical co-joined twins who don't present much of a challenge to Ator but there is also a fire-breathing dragon to contend with. Ator hacks it to pieces and is able to make the requisite offering to the gods.

Ator then proceeds to the trap-filled lair where Dejanira is held. He revives Dejanira with a kiss but also incurs the wrath of the gods (despite his previous offering). Volcanoes erupt and the cavern starts crashing down, prompting an Indiana Jones-style race to safety.

They head to a tavern where Ator gets into a fight over a prostitute. The three of them are thrown out and the prostitute reveals that she has been cursed by the gods to be a prostitute forever. The curse will only be lifted when a man looks at her, not as a woman, but as a mother. When Ator reveals his name, they both realize that they are mother and son and the curse is lifted. Ator's mother then withers into an old woman and dies.

Ator and Dejanira head towards the Land of the East, presumably hoping to outrun the gods' ire. Dejanira is captured by men belonging to Gunther (Donal O'Brien), a local ruler with a nasty case of face boils. He also has a nasty habit of turning women (and pets) who spurn him into plaster models. Naturally, Ator isn't about to let that happen to Dejanira so the movie rounds up with a castle infiltration and a damsel rescue.

This rather disjointed third act involving a villain that had nothing to do with previous events is due to the whole movie being a rehash of Wagner's *The Ring of the Nibelungs*. In that story, the hero Siegfried re-forges his father's sword, slays a dwarf (and a dragon), rescues a Valkyrie from a ring of fire and then goes on to have further adventures involving a royal family headed by a king called Gunther.

D'Amato's attempt to completely write over the third Ator movie is evident by *Quest for the Mighty Sword*'s alternative title of '*Ator III: The Hobgoblin*'. In some European countries, it was rather confusingly marketed as '*Troll 3*'. D'Amato had already produced an entirely unrelated *Troll 2* and reused one of its costumes for the character of Grindl. Incidentally, *Troll 2* was an attempt to hoodwink audiences into thinking it was a sequel to the 1986 hit *Troll* which starred *The Neverending Story*'s Noah Hathaway as (I kid you not) Harry Potter, a boy who battles a grotesque little creature that has invaded his San Francisco home.

CONCLUSION

The machismo of the Reagan era softened as the nineties dawned on a more cynical decade in which action stars started to show a more sensitive side. Actors like Harrison Ford often portrayed family men forced to take action in extreme situations while Keanu Reeves, Will Smith and Nicholas Cage showed that being built like a tank wasn't such a big deal anymore. Even Arnold Schwarzenegger began to appear in more family friendly movies like *Kindergarten Cop* (1990) while parodying his earlier career in *Last Action Hero* (1993). As for sword and sorcery movies, the genre went from boom to bust and practically sizzled out in the early nineties. The image of a half-naked woman clinging to the bulging thighs of an oiled up, muscular barbarian with a big sword and bigger hair, became an object of ridicule and was seen as a relic of an outdated and sexist fad.

The transition wasn't sudden however, and there was a certain tapering off. A Beastmaster sequel appeared in 1991 (*Beastmaster II: Through the Portal of Time*) which had Marc Singer's Dar wind up in present day Los Angeles and the franchise eventually wound up as a short-lived TV incarnation. *Highlander* had a run of sequels from 1991 to 2007 and also enjoyed some success as a TV series.

In fact, TV became the home of sword and sorcery in the nineties. Glossy shows that didn't take themselves too seriously like *Hercules: The Legendary Journeys* starring Kevin Sorbo and its spinoff, *Xena: Warrior Princess* starring Lucy Lawless mixed humor with episodic adventure. Kevin Sorbo would go on to play Kull in *Kull the Conqueror* (1997) which rehashed the script for an axed Conan sequel but was met with little praise. 1997 also saw Conan get his own TV series starring Ralf Möller (*Conan the Adventurer*) which was similar in style and tone to *Hercules* and *Xena*.

As Cannon's familiar chrome logo vanished from screens for good, it became clear that the movie industry had changed. The rise of the film festival circuit in the early nineties created a boom in indie movies that began to be big box office draws. Young talent didn't have to put in the years churning out cheap exploitation movies for the likes of Roger Corman anymore. As the Tarantinos and the Soderburghs of this new generation of filmmakers proved, low budget filmmaking no longer equated trashy genre pictures.

Italian cinema had found its feet again too. A new generation of young filmmakers were returning some critical acclaim to Italian cinema in the early nineties. The international success of *Nuovo Cinema Paradiso* (1988), which won the Academy Award for Best Foreign Film in 1990, continued with *Mediterraneo* (1991) and *Il Postino* (1994). The era of the Italian cash in and cheap exploitation movie was over.

Sword and sorcery had simply fallen out of fashion. Oversaturation was certainly a factor and it wasn't just movies that had given people barbarian fatigue by the mid-eighties. The publishing industry was glutted with Conan pastiches and knockoffs. Quality and originality went out the window and people were starting to notice. Terry Pratchett's 1985 novel *The Color of Magic* (the inauguration of his lengthy Discworld series), was a blatant parody of a stale genre that had begun to draw derision.

The fall of the slim sword and sorcery novel was eclipsed by the rise of the high fantasy doorstopper. The success of Terry Brooks' *The Sword of Shannara* in 1977 had ushered in an era of lengthy series concerning elves, dragons and magical quests in the Tolkien mold. *The Belgariad* by David Eddings followed in 1982, and the Dragonlance series by Margaret Weis and Tracy Hickman in 1984. Writers who made their bones churning out Conan stories in the seventies and eighties jumped genre like Robert Jordan whose first book in his fourteen-volume *The Wheel of Time* series appeared in 1990. By then, it seemed that if a fantasy novel wasn't part of a trilogy or a multi-tome series, publishers weren't interested.

While fantasy as a whole has enjoyed a resurgence on the screen ever since the phenomenal success of Peter Jackson's *The Lord of the Rings* trilogy in 2001, sword and sorcery hasn't really returned with it. Repeated failures at bringing Arnold Schwarzenegger back as Conan prompted filmmakers to start over but a 2011 remake with Jason Momoa in the role failed to make much of a splash. There have been underground favorites like the 2006 Russian movie *Wolfhound*, based on the Volkodav series of books by Maria Semyonova as well as a Solomon Kane movie starring James Purfoy in 2009. *The Witcher*, Netflix's 2019 series based on the books by Andrzej Sapkowski was a high profile effort but the influence of *Game of Thrones* is evident in its convoluted plot leaving us to wonder if high fantasy is what audiences would rather have.

We now live in an age where nostalgia is a hot commodity and remakes and sequels to long dead franchises are the norm. There have been few attempts to do anything new with sword and sorcery and, for a genre that has such stringent definitions, not to mention a cinematic heritage that is more likely to elicit mirth than awe from modern audiences, it is unclear how long we will have to wait for a fresh take that lands squarely within the genre *and* comes close to the success of *Conan the Barbarian*.

Those who came of age in the 1980s and enjoyed the movies discussed in this book are in their middle years now and pop culture's current obsession with the eighties (manifested in things like *Stranger Things* and *Ready Player One*), is a testament to our fondness for the relics of our past. Wanting new and original takes is natural. Genres stagnate and must explore new ground to stay vibrant but there is also a wonderful pleasure to be found in simply enjoying the things we once had.

One way genres can evolve is by looking at themselves through the prism of the past, reveling in their tropes and toying with their conventions. My upcoming novel *Bladereaper and the Game Zone of Fate* is an homage to both the 1980s and the sword and sorcery genre. It switches between the fantasy world of Skaldheim, where the titular Bladereaper (a muscular barbarian warrior) battles a wicked cult that has resurrected an ancient evil, and our own world circa 1987, where teenaged Billy Kurgen (a fan of fantasy movies and heavy metal) struggles with bullies and a fractured family. The link between the two worlds is a video arcade game called *Bladereaper*, which gradually consumes Billy as he comes to realize that the fate of one world will be decided in another.

Part sword and sorcery yarn, part suburban coming-of-age tale, *Bladereaper and the Game Zone of Fate* is a thrilling slice of '80s nostalgia in the spirit of *Stranger Things* and *Ready Player One*. Available now.

APPENDIX - TIMELINE

1896

- *The Well at World's End* and *The Wood Beyond the World* by William Morris are published and are the first examples of 'secondary world' novels.

1905

- *Lieutenant Gullivar Jones: His Vacation* (later published as Gulliver of Mars) by Edwin L. Arnold is published and is one of the first examples of the 'sword and planet' genre.

1912

- *Under the Moons of Mars* (later published as *A Princess of Mars*) by Edgar Rice Burroughs is serialized in All-Story magazine. The novel influences many sword and sorcery and science fiction writers and is considered the quintessential sword and planet novel.

1922

- *The Worm Ouroboros* by E. R. Eddison is published; an early fantasy novel that inspires J. R. R. Tolkien.

1923

- J. C. Henneberger sets up *Weird Tales*, a magazine devoted to horror and fantasy fiction. It features the stories of many early sword and sorcery writers like Robert E. Howard, Clark Ashton Smith, C. L. Moore, and Henry Kuttner.

1924

- *The King of Elfland's Daughter* by Lord Dunsany is published; an early fantasy classic.

1928
- The first Solomon Kane story (*Red Shadows*) by Robert E. Howard is published in *Weird Tales*

1929
- The First Kull story (*The Shadow Kingdom*) by Robert E. Howard is published in *Weird Tales*.

1932
- The first Conan story (*The Phoenix on the Sword*) by Robert E. Howard is published in *Weird Tales*

1934
- The first Jirel of Joiry story (*Black God's Kiss*) by C. L. Moore is published in *Weird Tales*.
- King Features Syndicate begins printing Alex Raymond's *Flash Gordon* newspaper strip.

1938
- The first Elak of Atlantis story (*Thunder in the Dawn*) by Henry Kuttner is published in *Weird Tales*.

1939
- The first Fafhrd and the Gray Mouser story (*Two Sought Adventure*) by Fritz Leiber is published in *Unknown*.

1950
- *The Dying Earth* by Jack Vance is published and later influences *Dungeons and Dragons*.
- Robert E. Howard's only Conan novel (*The Hour of the Dragon*) is published under the name *Conan the Conqueror* by Gnome Press fourteen years after its author's suicide.

1953

- *The Sword of Rhiannon* by Leigh Brackett is published.
- *The Tritonian Ring* by L. Sprague de Camp is published.

1954

- *The Fellowship of the Ring* by J. R. R. Tolkien is published in the UK.
- *The Broken Sword* by Poul Anderson is published.

1955

- *The Two Towers* and *The Return of the King* by J. R. R. Tolkien are published in the UK.

1957

- *Hercules*, the first 'peplum' movie starring Steve Reeves is released.

1958

- *The 7ᵗʰ Voyage of Sinbad*; the first of several sword and sorcery movies featuring Ray Harryhausen's monsters is released.

1961

- *Three Hearts and Three Lions* by Poul Anderson is published and later influences *Dungeons and Dragons*.
- Fritz Leiber coins the term 'sword and sorcery' in *Amra*, Vol. 2 No. 16.
- Michael Moorcock's Elric character first appears in the short story *The Dreaming City* published in *Science Fantasy #47*.

1964

- *Jason and the Argonauts* is released.

1965

- Ballantine publishes *The Lord of the Rings* trilogy in paperback in the US to huge success, making fantasy fiction a viable option in the eyes of publishers.

- *The Wizard of Lemuria* by Lin Carter is published, the first of his Thongor the Barbarian series.

1966

- Lancer Paperbacks begin publishing Robert E. Howard's Conan stories with Frank Frazetta's cover illustrations.

1967

- *Tarnsman of Gor* by John Norman is published.

1968

- *Brak the Barbarian* by John Jakes is published.

1969

- *Kothar - Barbarian Swordsman* by Gardner F. Fox is published.
- Lin Carter begins editing Adult Fantasy Series anthologies for Ballantine which collects older stories by Lord Dunsany, Clark Ashton Smith and William Morris among others.

1970

- *Ill Met in Lankhmar* by Fritz Leiber is published in the *Magazine of Fantasy and Science Fiction* being an origin story for his Fafhrd and the Gray Mouser characters. It wins the Nebula Award for Best Novella.
- The first Kane novel (*Darkness Weaves with Many Shades*) by Karl Edward Wagner is published.
- *Swords Against Tomorrow* is published, an anthology of works by various members of SAGA (the Swordsmen and Sorcerer's Guild of America).

- Marvel Comics begins its *Conan the Barbarian* series.

1971
- Marvel Comics begins its *Kull the Conqueror* series.

1973
- The first volume of *Flashing Swords!* by Lin Carter collects more work from the members of SAGA.
- Red Sonja makes her first appearance in Marvel's *Conan the Barbarian #23*.
- Marvel Comics begins its adaption of Lin Carter's *Thongor of Lemuria*.
- DC Comics begins its *Sword of Sorcery* series featuring the adventures of Fritz Leiber's Fafhrd and the Gray Mouser.

1974
- *Dungeons and Dragons* is created by Gary Gygax and Dave Arneson.
- *The Golden Voyage of Sinbad* is released.
- The first Imaro stories by Charles R. Saunders are published in *Dark Fantasy*. The character is the first example of a non-white sword and sorcery hero.
- Marvel Comics begins its more adult *The Savage Sword of Conan* series through its imprint company, Curtis Magazines.

1975
- DC Comics begins its *Claw the Unconquered* series.

1977
- *Advanced Dungeons and Dragons* is created by Gary Gygax.

- *Star Wars* is released, paving the way for a boom in fantasy and adventure films in the following decade.
- *Sinbad and the Eye of the Tiger* is released.
- *The Sword of Shannara* by Terry Brooks is published and is the first fantasy novel to make the New York Times bestseller list, indicating an increasing acceptance of fantasy fiction as a whole into mainstream literature.
- Marvel Comics begins its *Red Sonja* series.

1978
- Ralph Bakshi's animated adaption of *The Lord of the Rings* is released.

1979
- The first of Robert Asprin's popular 'shared world' anthologies *Thieves World* is published, including work by Poul Anderson, Marion Zimmer Bradley and others.

REFERENCES

1. Leiber, Fritz. "Letter." *Amra,* Vol. 2 No. 16. Arlington, VA: George H. Scithers, July 1961.

2. Carter, Lin. *Flashing Swords! Volume 1.* Edited by Carter. N. Doubleday, 1973.

3. Murphy, Brian. *Flame and Crimson: A History of Sword-and-Sorcery.* Bob McLain Media, 2020.

4. Strahan, Johnathan and Anders, Lou. *Swords & Dark Magic: The New Sword and Sorcery.* Subterranean, 2010.

5. https://www.dreadcentral.com/news/32110 6/exclusive-posthumous-interview-with-david-paul-of-the-barbarian-brothers/

6. Kline, Sally. *George Lucas: Interviews (Conversations with Filmmakers Series).* University Press of Mississippi, 1999

7. Curti, Roberto. *Diabolika: Supercriminals, Superheroes and the Comic Book Universe in Italian Cinema.* Midnight Marquee Press, Inc, 2016

8. https://www.theguardian.com/film/2016/j ul/05/highlander-how-we-made-sean-connery-christopher-lambert-russell-mulcahy-interview

9. https://www.cbr.com/he-man-conan-toy-tie-in/

10. https://www.dailydot.com/irl/gor-gorean-slaves-history/

11. Mann, Dave, *Harry Alan Towers: The Transnational Career of a Cinematic Contrarian*. McFarland, 2014.

12. Mann, Dave, *Harry Alan Towers: The Transnational Career of a Cinematic Contrarian*. McFarland, 2014. pg. 130

13. Mann, Dave, *Harry Alan Towers: The Transnational Career of a Cinematic Contrarian*. McFarland, 2014. pg. 128

14. https://www.upi.com/Archives/1988/10/11/Cannon-Film-withdraws-from-South-Africa/4648592545600/

15. Ratner, B. Packer, J. Fury, V (Producers), & Hartley, M. (Director). (2014). *Electric Boogaloo: The Wild, Untold Story of Cannon Films*. Australia, U.S.A.: RatPac Documentary Films.

16. Waddell, Calum. *Jack Hill: The Exploitation and Blaxploitation Master, Film by Film*. McFarland, 2009.

17. Falicov, Tamara L. "U.S.-Argentine Co-productions, 1982-1990: Roger Corman, Aries Productions, "Schlockbuster" Movies, and the International Market." *Film & History: An Interdisciplinary Journal of Film and Television Studies*, vol. 34 no. 1, 2004, p. 31-38. Project MUSE, doi:10.1353/flm.2004.0015

18. Gray, Beverly. *Roger Corman: Blood-Sucking Vampires, Flesh-Eating Cockroaches, and Driller Killers*. AZ Ferris Publications, 2012

19. "Log Entries." *Starlog Number 072*, July. 1983.

20. https://podcastingthemsoftly.com/2016/11/15/is-that-your-first-name-or-your-last-name-remembering-deathstalker-2-with-jim-wynorski-by-kent-hill/

21. The New York Times, April 30, 1990, Section C, Page 11/ https://www.nytimes.com/1990/04/30/movies/east-bloc-film-makers-have-liberty-to-say-what-they-truly-mean.html

22. Gray, Beverly. *Roger Corman: Blood-Sucking Vampires, Flesh-Eating Cockroaches, and Driller Killers*. AZ Ferris Publications, 2012

23. https://www.nanarland.com/interview/interview-enzogcastellari-page-3.html

Printed in Great Britain
by Amazon

27284358R00111